CAMBRIDGE MUSIC HA

Bartók: Concerto for Orchestra

CAMBRIDGE MUSIC HANDBOOKS

GENERAL EDITOR Julian Rushton

Cambridge Music Handbooks provide accessible introductions to major musical works, written by the most informed commentators in the field. With the concert-goer, performer and student in mind, the books present essential information on the historical and musical context, the composition, and the performance and reception history of each work, or group of works, as well as critical discussion of the music.

Other published titles

Bartók: Concerto for Orchestra

David Cooper

Lecturer in Music, University of Leeds

CAMBRIDGE UNIVERSITY PRESS
Cambridge, New York, Melbourne, Madrid, Cape Town, Singapore, São Paulo

Cambridge University Press
The Edinburgh Building, Cambridge CB2 2RU, UK

Published in the United States of America by Cambridge University Press, New York

www.cambridge.org
Information on this title: www.cambridge.org/9780521480048

© Cambridge University Press 1996

First published 1996
Reprinted 2004

A catalogue record for this publication is available from the British Library

Library of Congress Cataloguing in Publication data

Cooper, David, 1956–
Bartók, Concerto for Orchestra / David Cooper
p.   cm. – (Cambridge music handbooks)
Includes bibliographical references and index.
ISBN 0 521 48004 3 hardback . – ISBN 0 521 48505 3 paperback
1. Bartók, Béla, 1881 1945. Concertos, orchestra.
I. Title. II. Series.
ML410.B26C66 1996
784.2′186-dc20   95-21614 CIP MN

ISBN-13 978-0-521-48004-8 hardback
ISBN-10 0-521-48004-3 hardback

ISBN-13 978-0-521-48505-0 paperback
ISBN-10 0-521-48505-3 paperback

Transferred to digital printing 2005

Contents

Contents

Abbreviations and acknowledgements

The following abbreviations are used in the notes (full details of publications are in the select bibliography):

BBE *Béla Bartók Essays*, ed. Benjamin Suchoff
BBL *Béla Bartók Letters*, ed. János Demény
BC   *The Bartók Companion*, ed. Malcolm Gillies
BR   *Bartók Remembered*, ed. Malcolm Gillies

Pitches are notated using the ASA rather than the Helmholtz system. The following table converts between the two systems.

Helmholtz	ASA
CC	C_1
C	C_2
c	C_3
c^1	C_4
c^2	C_5
c^3	C_6
c^4	C_7

Musical example 3(b) is reprinted by permission of Universal Edition (London) Ltd. All rights in the USA controlled by Boosey & Hawkes Inc., New York.

Musical examples 6 and 28 are taken from *Serbo-Croatian Folk Songs* by Béla Bartók and Albert B. Lord. Copyright © 1951 by Columbia University Press. Reprinted with permission of the publisher.

Musical example 8 is taken from *Hungarian Folk Music* by Béla Bartók and is reproduced by permission of Oxford University Press.

All other musical examples are reproduced by permission of Boosey & Hawkes Music Publishers Ltd.

Bartók's explanation (Appendix (a)) is copyright © the Boston Symphony Orchestra, Inc., and is reprinted by permission.

I would like to acknowledge the kind assistance of the staff of the Boston Symphony Orchestra archive who supplied copies of early reviews and other material, and to those of the hire library of Boosey & Hawkes for access to their records of European performances. I am grateful to Peter Franklin for his translation of the Hesse diary-entry in the introduction, his help in translating the Fricsay in Chapter 5 and for many stimulating lunch-time discussions. Especial thanks must go to Julian Rushton for reading the draft and supplying many helpful comments and corrections.

1

Introduction

... this other music of today, the music of Bartók! Chaos in place of Cosmos, confusion in place of order, scattered clouds of aural sensation in place of clarity and shape, fortuitous proportions and a renunciation of architecture in place of structure and controlled development. Yet this too was masterly. Even beautiful, moving, sublime, wonderfully gifted! ... And all the more beautiful and irresistible by virtue of its being precisely the music of our time: an expression of our experience, our view of life, our strengths and our weaknesses. It expresses us and our questionable life-styles while also affirming us. Like us, this music knows the beauty of dissonance and pain; the many scales of fractional and varied tones, the overthrow and relativization of morals and established modes of thought. No less than us does it know the yearning for the paradises of order and security, of logic and of harmony.[1]

Hermann Hesse's diary-entry of 15 May 1955, in response to a radio broadcast that morning of the Concerto for Orchestra and a concerto grosso by Handel, captures the essence of Bartók's music, with its precarious tightrope balance between urban art music and rural popular music, tonality and atonality, chaos and order. The conventional musical analyst will probably reject Hesse's opinions of the structural fortuity of the work as the value judgement of an amateur. Yet Hesse's assessment avoids the tendency to normalize Bartók's music which is so prevalent among professional commentators today, albeit according to a number of different systems of analysis. By rejecting the closed listening that can result from dogmatic adherence to a single analytic system, Hesse opens his ears to the music as phenomenon, and hears within it the imprint of the chaos which gives meaning to our lives.

It is widely accepted that Bartók achieved a synthesis in his music,[2] in which the oppositions alluded to above, among others, have been neutralized within a unified musical structure. However, the very plurality of the strategies used to 'explain' this synthesis and the unity which results from it may suggest to the sceptic that the cohesion and congruity which the normalizing critic observes may well be illusory. Perhaps we should admire Bartók's music as much for its ability to accommodate, as for its tendency to assimilate

1

difference, for its admission of the coexistence of disparate materials, as much as their integration.

As Hesse implies, it is the fragmentary nature of the music which makes it such a potent metaphor for, and reflection of, contemporary life. He hears in it an allusive quality, which intimates both the world of nature, and the world of man in its avoidance of regularity and symmetry. Its soundworld had

the beauty of the silvery scores that are fantastically drawn by the summer-wind in grass; the beauty of a swirl of snowflakes, or of the short-lived play of dramatic evening-light over the surface of sand-dunes. So too did it have the beauty of those just-lost sounds that one can't pin down to laughter or sobbing – such sounds as one might hear while travelling: half-waking for the first time in a foreign city, in a strange room and bed. One would love to know what each was, but there is no time, so quickly and restlessly do they tumble upon each other. Just so does this richly sensual, colourful, painfully beautiful music ripple, laugh, sob, groan, grumble and gambol on its way – without logic, without stasis; all movement, all beautiful, fading transitoriness.

Given the difficult circumstances surrounding the composition of the Concerto, and its subsequent popular success, it is too easy to regard it as a compromise of the composer's musical integrity, a mere money-spinner for his wife Ditta after his death. The musical language of the work is, however, the culmination of a process of simplification and crystallization of Bartók's style in terms of density of dissonance and increased use of triadic harmony,[3] a process which began around 1930, after a period of experimentation which had seen the composition of such works as *The Miraculous Mandarin,* the two Violin Sonatas, the relatively rebarbative middle pair of String Quartets, and the First Piano Concerto. This process reflects Bartók's conviction, expressed in print in 1938, that contemporary music 'ought to be directed at the present time to the search for that which we will call "inspired simplicity"'.[4]

The Concerto is historically embedded in a world in crisis. Written at the turning point of the Second World War, it forms the most powerful of Requiems, one that perhaps only an atheist could have written. It is a lament for man's inhumanity to man, but also a positive vision of a world in a kind of harmony in which chaos and order, the primeval enemies, are held in dynamic equilibrium.

2

Background

'In the name of Nature, Art and Science . . .'[1]

Béla Bartók invoked his personal trinity in 1907, at the age of twenty-six, in a letter to his friend the violinist Stefi Geyer, and for the rest of his life devoted himself to its veneration with a commitment and conviction that matched the intensity of his early rejection of conventional religious belief.[2] For Bartók, the music of the uneducated rural peasantry which he began studying seriously in 1905 was as much a manifestation of nature as the butterflies, insects and alpine flowers he collected:

Peasant music, in the strict sense of the word, must be regarded as a natural phenomenon; the forms in which it manifests itself are due to the instinctive *transforming power* of a community entirely devoid of erudition. It is just as much a natural phenomenon as, for instance, the various manifestations of Nature in fauna and flora. Correspondingly it has in its individual parts an absolute artistic perfection, a perfection in miniature forms which – one might say – is equal to the perfection of a musical masterpiece of the largest proportions. It is the classical model of how to express an idea musically in the most concise form, with the greatest simplicity of means, with freshness and life, briefly yet completely and properly proportioned.[3]

There is a strange inverse relationship between Bartók's construct of the innately artistic peasantry which produces melodies that are models of perfection (though individual peasants are not to be credited with the composition of songs or instrumental music, but rather with their modification and variation),[4] and Heinrich Schenker's concept of the unique, divinely inspired improvising genius who 'composes out' the fundamental structure, which is itself derived from nature. In both constructs, the musicians are effectively deprived of agency, and form a medium through which culture is spontaneously transmitted, their role being essentially passive. Whilst such a view, redolent as it is of a fairly conventional nineteenth-century Romantic idealism, is deeply problematic, it is consistently and unambiguously expressed throughout Bartók's writings. Leibowitz suggests that Bartók was attracted by a freedom, asymmetry and perhaps even a chaos which he could

3

discern in rural music, and which mirrored his own musical interests and predilections.[5] It is possible that he heard in its 'eternal changeableness' a reflection of the arbitrariness and variability of nature,[6] but it is clear that he particularly admired it for its total 'absence of sentimentality and exaggeration of expression',[7] features which became characteristics of his own compositional language.

Bartók perceived a dichotomy between the 'natural' unconscious artistry of peasant music (especially of an older kind untainted by civilization) and the artificiality of an urban folk music whose function was 'to furnish entertainment and to satisfy the musical needs of those whose sensibilities are of a low order'.[8] The non-alienated peasantry who still retained the crafts and customs of their ancestors, and whose lives were sustained by the fruit of their own labour, provided the last link to the older, innate musical culture, and it was from this class (which was probably already something of an anachronism when he started collecting folk music) that he transcribed the songs which were to have the greatest influence on his own musical output.[9]

He naïvely held the peasantry to be peace-loving, apolitical beings in harmony with both the natural world and the peoples of neighbouring countries, and felt they were drawn, against their best instincts, into conflicts and wars, betrayed by their corrupt urban masters. Their songs expressed a kind of non-political nationalism which was devoid of chauvinism and competition, for 'where politics begin, art and science come to an end, equity and good faith cease to exist'.[10] Such a view informs his own mature music, for it is rarely conventionally nationalistic, but draws on folkloric influences from a wide range of musical dialects including Hungarian, Romanian, Slovakian, Serbo-Croatian, North African and Turkish.[11]

In the ethnomusicological hagiography, Bartók's name is still revered as one of the founding fathers of the objective study of popular music, though there are revisionist voices which suggest that his importance has been somewhat overrated. As early as 1931, in a review of *Hungarian Folk Music*, the composer and critic Bernard Van Dieren poured scorn on Bartók the 'scientist'. In a splenetic and scornful attack, he pilloried Bartók for being

so bewitched by the glamour of supposed 'scientific research' that he expends his valuable time on work that any efficient clerk might in a couple of years be trained to do. He aspires to rank with the paleontologist with his stones and bones, or the biologist with his microscope, diatoma, and protozoa.[12]

Van Dieren's basic criticism in this review (which at times is dazzlingly off the wall) is that Bartók's research is not properly scientific at all, but trivial hack-work which merely presents data, and does not use it either as 'an introduction to a new working method' or 'for reference, with deductions leading to a system or theory from which he could claim personal credit'.[13] His tone, moreover, suggests that he believed that even the attempt to study music of a 'racial popular idiom' was effectively worthless and irrelevant.

Bartók believed that one of the main functions of folk-music research was to help to trace the common ancestry of races who were physically separated from each other and whose music contained common features.[14] Such a goal, requiring the collection of vast quantities of raw data from many ethnic sources, implies that Bartók's brand of ethnomusicology is indeed a form of palaeontology, and can be best considered as being allied to various branches of the social sciences including linguistics, and social and cultural anthropology. As Lenoir has observed, there are parallels between Bartók's methodology and that of structuralists such as Propp and Lévi-Strauss in the field of mythology, and Jakobson in linguistics.[15]

Although he had no formal advanced training as a scientist, Bartók seems to have exhibited considerable acumen in both physics and mathematics at school, and developed an amateur interest in astronomy, the natural sciences and technology. In terms of his 'scientific' approach, he was more of a Rosalind Franklin than a John Watson.[16] The hallmarks of the transcriptions and comparative analyses of the materials he collected were fastidiousness and rigour, characteristics which are exemplified in the extreme detail with which he notated the rhythmic and melodic parameters of the music. His method, which was closer to that of a photographer than a sketch-artist, was contrived to present the music in as accurate and objective a way as possible, and avoid subjective interpretation wherever feasible, though he made it clear that this was very often difficult.[17] Each transcription is thus the representation of a single performance by an individual peasant, rather than an averaged-out illustration of a class of melodies, like a single butterfly with its own distinct phenotype pinned to a board by a lepidopterist.

The method of taxonomy adopted by Bartók was adapted from that of the Finnish musicologist Ilmari Krohn, and subjected to various revisions in the course of his career. It provides for the discrimination of musical 'genotypes' by such essential features as scale type, form, number of melodic lines, cadential note of each line, syllabic and rhythmic structure, and range. A song or instrumental melody could thus be reduced to a fairly simple formula or structure, and be tabulated for comparison with other transcriptions in the corpus from the same or other regions.

Bartók's writings do not indicate that the function of folk-music research was to preserve it by simply disseminating it to the urban proletariat. The precision and visual complexity of the transcriptions, with their rhythmic quantization levels of as little as a demisemiquaver or quintuplet semiquaver, and their microtonal inflections, often make them almost unreadable as performance scores; indeed it is questionable if any musician would wish to reproduce or realize such highly contingent performances, dependent as they are on the psychology and physiology of their original executants, their social function, and other specific prevailing conditions. They were to be regarded more as examples of natural form, or archetypes of organic musical practice which could provide the music student with material for imitation and emulation, and which could even have an analogous role to the Bach chorales conventionally used as models in academic institutions.[18] Whilst he made very many arrangements of actual peasant music for voice and piano, chorus, violin, and piano, these were the work of a lapidary who has polished the gems until they have lost their natural roughness, and set them as jewellery – domestic ornaments which are no longer intimately tied to the culture from which they sprang.

It was through the medium of 'art music' that the spirit of peasant music was to be retained:

the pure folk music can be considered as a natural phenomenon influencing higher art music, as bodily properties perceptible with the eye are for the fine arts, or the phenomena of life are for the poet. This influence is most effective for the musician if he acquaints himself with folk music in the form in which it lives, in unbridled strength, amidst the lower people, and not by means of inanimate collections of folk music which anyway lack adequate diatonic symbols capable of restoring their minute nuances and throbbing life.[19]

Ironically, the very act of notation freezes the music and destroys the 'essence . . . which enables it to awake the emotions in the soul of the composer',[20] just as the administration of chloroform to a butterfly kills what is so attractive about it – its freedom to interact with the rest of the natural world.

The apparently condescending tone he adopts should not be misunderstood – Bartók was no patrician aloofly admiring the peasantry as one might appreciate a herd of prize cattle; he honestly felt that their lifestyle was more valuable and authentic than that of the city. He seems to have been ill-at-ease with both the Hungarian aristocracy and the generally pro-German middle classes, and adopted the accoutrements of the 'lower people', delighting in their hand-carved furniture, embroidery and instruments.[21] But he could never, as a sophisticated outsider and observer, be wholly accepted within their culture. Instead, their culture was to be transplanted and absorbed into middle-class art music by composers who displayed 'great creative talent',[22] to bear fruit in an authentic national style, in a process which was analogous to that of the development of the Classical style from an amalgamation of Austro-German 'popular' music and its 'serious' counterpart. Bartók implies that the musical style which makes the best use of the peasant music is the one in which the composer does not quote from, or even imitate, folk music, but in which he uses it as a 'musical mother tongue',[23] the extremes of the 'great artistic genius' and 'illiterate peasant' becoming united in a synthesis of high and low art.

Zoltán Kodály, Bartók's compatriot, fellow ethnomusicologist and collaborator, and long-time friend, saw the strands of Bartók's trinity as being inextricably interwoven, for his performance and compositional activities were informed by his scientific work which in turn was enriched by his musical artistry:

For the roots of science and art are the same. Each, in its own way, reflects the world. The basic conditions: sharp powers of observation, precise expression of the life observed, and raising it to a higher synthesis. And the foundation of scientific and artistic greatness is also the same: just man, *vir justus*.[24]

The sources of the mature style – the orchestral music from *Kossuth* to the Second Piano Concerto

The compositional style of Bartók's late teens shows many of the influences that other composers of his generation would have shared, namely that of Brahms, Liszt and Wagner, the latter two composers becoming the subject of a detailed and enthusiastic study whilst he was a student at the Budapest Academy of Music between 1899 and 1903. In 1902 he attended the Hungarian première of Richard Strauss's symphonic tone poem *Also sprach Zarathustra* and was bowled over by it, believing it to hold 'the seeds of a new life'.[25] Later in 1902 he transcribed Strauss's *Ein Heldenleben* for solo piano, performing it on 26 January 1903 in the Vienna Tonkünstlerverein to considerable public acclaim.

The soil which initially ripened the seed sown by Strauss's works was that of Hungarian nationalism, which Bartók seems to have adopted as a political credo around 1902–3.[26] In doing so, he was reflecting a chauvinism that had been developing over the preceding years, which had been fostered by the

Hungarian ruling classes in the interests of promoting political and economic autonomy, and which, according to Ujfalussy,[27] was essentially divisive in nature in that it encouraged antagonism between the native and non-native Hungarian working classes. It was a brand of nationalism that had no role for the essentially marginalized peasantry, founded as it was on the notion of the aristocracy forming the entire 'Hungarian nation'.[28] Bartók felt that the nationalist ideals espoused by politicians should be adopted by the whole population, but rejected such demonstrations against Austrian rule as the commonplace refusal of people to sing the Austrian anthem 'Gott erhalte', believing them to be unhelpful to the Magyar cause. However, he felt that it was imperative that Hungarians should 'speak in a foreign language only when absolutely necessary',[29] properly to display their national pride.

The musical outcome of this nationalistic enthusiasm was *Kossuth*. This symphonic poem in ten sections based on the career of the lower nobleman Lajos Kossuth,[30] the leader of the Hungarian cause in the 1848 revolution, was composed between April and May 1903, and orchestrated in the summer of that year; Bartók considered it to be Hungarian in every way.[31] The Hungarian quality to which Bartók alludes derives from the essentially petty-aristocratic pseudo-folk *verbunkos* tradition which arose in the middle of the eighteenth century as an accompaniment to military recruitment ceremonies. It was moulded from an amalgam of musical styles, high and low, and from a disparate range of national sources, and was mainly disseminated by gypsy musicians. Stereotypical features of the *verbunkos* style include: the use of the so-called gypsy or 'Hungarian' scale with its idiosyncratic augmented seconds between the third and fourth notes and between the sixth and seventh notes (Ex. 1), a curt cambiata-like cadential figure (bokázó); a wide melodic tessitura with flamboyant decoration; and the alternation between slow (lassú) and fast (friss) tempi.[32] Whilst Liszt's *Hungarian Rhapsodies* and Brahms's *Hungarian Dances* are probably the most familiar examples of the transplantation of the *verbunkos* tradition into nineteenth-century art music,[33] it is in the works of the Hungarian Romantics such as Ferenc Erkel in opera, and Mihály Mosonyi in instrumental music, that this style is most self-consciously adopted and developed. In his later music, Bartók reassimilated the *verbunkos* tradition, particularly in *Contrasts* and the Sixth String Quartet. The third idea of the *Introduzione* of the Concerto for Orchestra, which reappears in the *Elegia* (see Chapter 4, Ex. 10), for example, is a stylized *verbunkos* gesture.

The *Rhapsody* Op. 1 for piano and orchestra (1904), and the First Suite for Orchestra (1905) whose five-movement structure foreshadows the Concerto

Ex. 1   The gypsy scale

for Orchestra, retain the influence of the *verbunkos*, though by 1905 Bartók was much less interested in Strauss, and was rediscovering the works of Liszt, which 'after being stripped of their mere external brilliance which I did not like, revealed to me the true essence of composing'.[34] His discovery of an autochthonous Hungarian music in 1905,[35] encouraged by Zoltán Kodály, had less of an initially dramatic consequence than his Straussian epiphany; in the third movement of the serenade-like Second Suite for Orchestra (1905–7) a melody appears whose structure bears the influence of the old-style peasant music,[36] and in the finale a pentatonic folk-like fragment emerges, which hints at the new compositional possibilities that peasant music might nurture, whilst remaining firmly rooted in a conventional late-Romantic chromatic style.

The adoption of a style which bears the influences of peasant rather than gypsy music implies a political as well a musical change of heart on the part of Bartók,[37] for the peasant music which particularly interested him was the most ancient type, whose origins may have even predated the conquest of Hungary, and which was thus clearly detached from the musico-nationalistic status quo. As Frigyesi observes:

the recognition of peasant music was offensive because it called attention to the existence of a Hungarian art known only to the peasants, and hence independent of the upper classes, the nobility, and the gentry. Collectivity or spontaneity of musical culture was a similarly sensitive issue, since it was thought that the 'weeping-rejoicing' Gypsy music was the most characteristic and spontaneous expression of the Hungarian soul. . . . In a sense, Bartók and Kodály were taking away whatever was valued as 'national' in Gypsy music and transferring it to the peasant song, whose very existence had not previously been suspected. They undermined the notion that national character could be represented by one class and taken as the ultimate measure of value.[38]

Bartók's borrowings from peasant music are generally applied on the microscopic rather than macroscopic scale: he tends to adopt the scale forms, phrasings, metres, rhythms, or rough melodic contours of folk-sources (very rarely quoting verbatim from actual melodies in his large-scale works), and he often employs them within what initially appear to be conventional musical forms such as ternary or sonata form. Thus the peasant music, especially the

9

Ex. 2   The acoustic scale on C

'older' type, which is generally not rounded or 'architectural',[39] provides substitutes for the periods and sentences which articulate the thematic ideas of much eighteenth- and nineteenth-century music, and which themselves were often influenced by popular models. It also supplies several novel scale forms,[40] in particular one which is called the acoustic scale (because it is derived from the first sixteen harmonics of a harmonic series starting, in Example 2, on C) by the Hungarian musicologist Ernő Lendvai, and *heptatonia secunda* (or second seven-note system, parallel to the diatonic seven-note modes) by Lajos Bárdos.[41] The acoustic scale particularly dominates the finale of the Concerto for Orchestra.

In 1907 Bartók became interested in the music of Claude Debussy, noting in it ' "pentatonic phrases" similar in character to those contained in our peasant music'.[42] It may be reasonable to ascribe to Debussy's influence the appearance of the whole-tone scale, a formation which is not found as such in central European folk music, in the *Two Pictures* ('Images') for orchestra Op. 10 (1910), where it saturates the final section of the impressionistic first picture, 'In full flower', and strongly flavours the second, 'Village dance'. Whilst from this point on, whole-tone fragments are to be found in Bartók's oeuvre, including the second movement of the Concerto for Orchestra, none of the large-scale works is articulated by the unambiguous employment of this mode, its use being highly localized.

The slow–fast pairing used in *Two Pictures* is also to be found in the two large-scale theatrical works written in the period leading up to the First World War: the opera *Duke Bluebeard's Castle*, and the ballet *The Wooden Prince*.[43] *Duke Bluebeard's Castle* Op. 11 of 1911, with a libretto by Béla Balázs, the first fruit of Bartók's maturity, bears witness to the overwhelming influence of Hungarian peasant music without ever quoting a single original peasant melody. Whilst Debussy's *Pelléas et Mélisande* casts its unmistakable shadow, the opera's Hungarian quality is guaranteed by the pervasive influence of the Hungarian language on the vocal rhythms, and the sustained use of pentatonicism. In effect the opera is like a massive slow movement which forms a parabolic trajectory from dark, through light, then returning to darkness. In contrast, the ballet *The Wooden Prince*, which is concerned with the rights of passage of youthful love, as opposed to the dark aberrations of *Bluebeard*, is altogether brighter in mood. Its materials show a rather wider range of peasant influences than the opera, and vestigial traces of Romanian, Slovakian and Arab music can be noted as well as the purely Hungarian turns of phrase. It is a token of Bartók's affection for *Bluebeard* that the first idea of the *Introduzione* of the Concerto for Orchestra should bear a great similarity to the opening passage of the opera.

The use of autochthonous music within traditional forms can be seen as problematic, for, as Constant Lambert points out in a discussion about nineteenth-century Russian nationalism, what often results is not a synthesis but a struggle between competing styles:

Spiritually speaking, this struggle is symbolized by the contrast between the sonata and the fugue on one hand, types of aristocratic, international and intellectual expression, and the folk song and folk dance on the other, types of popular, national and instinctive expression. More technically speaking, it is due to the fact that folk songs – round which national expression in music centres – being already finished works of art with a line of their own, obstinately refuse to become links or component parts in the longer and more sweeping line demanded by the larger instrumental forms.[44]

Despite Bartók's avoidance of original folk song in his large-scale works, there is still a tension between the folk-modelled material and the rest of the musical context which is never fully resolved, and in a sense, it is the fracture which results from these competing styles rather than their synthesis which helps to propel the music.

His third theatrical work was the ballet *The Miraculous Mandarin*, composed between 1918 and 1919 and orchestrated in 1923, but not performed until 1926. This shows a marked intensification of his musical language both in terms of the level of dissonance and of chromaticism: the regular throughput of the pitches of the chromatic scale makes the work appear at some points to be virtually atonal. It may be that this more chromatic style was in part due to the influence of Schoenberg, whose music he had discovered in 1912 thanks to one of his piano pupils who had brought him a copy of the Three Piano Pieces Op. 11, and with whose harmony textbook (*Harmonielehre*) he was familiar. Although he regarded Schoenberg's music as being completely alienated from nature,[45] by which he meant that it was not influenced by peasant music (accounting for its difficulty and lack of popular success), he felt that it had exerted a profound effect, particularly on the younger generation of Hungarian composers.[46]

His attitude to atonality was ambiguous; writing in 1920 he suggested that his own music was moving in that direction, and that 'the ultimate objective of our endeavours is the unlimited and complete use of all extant, possible tonal material'.[47] He did not believe there to be a conflict between atonality and the use of triads or consonant intervals such as the major third, perfect fifth or octave, formations which were generally avoided by composers of the Second Viennese School because of their tonal implications. In later years, however, he denied that he was ever truly an atonal composer, preferring to see tonal centres, albeit attenuated in function, in all his works; he remarked, in the second of a series of lectures delivered at Harvard University in 1943, that his music was 'always based on a single fundamental tone, in its sections as well as its whole'.[48]

Ex. 3(a)   Arab scale from an instrumental melody
(transposed and enharmonically renotated from Bartók's original)[49]

Ex. 3(b)   *The Miraculous Mandarin* chase music from one bar after figure 62

Much of the chromaticism in *The Miraculous Mandarin* displays the impress of Arab music, particularly that of the region around Biskra in North Africa, which Bartók visited in the summer of 1913 to collect folk material. In the instrumental music of this district he discovered a number of exotic, non-diatonic scales with more than seven essential notes, such as Example 3(a).

This scale is particularly fertile as a source of melodic material, for it contains several forms of the pentatonic scale (C♯–D♯–F♯–G♯–A♯, C–E♭–F–A♭–B♭ and F♯–G♯–B–C♯–D♯), an octatonic segment of the type which pervades the Concerto for Orchestra (E♭–F–G♭–A♭–A), a chromatic segment (G♯–A–B♭–B–[C]–C♯), and two symmetrical segments (C–D♭–E♭–F–F♯ and F–[ ]–G♯–A–B♭–[ ]–C♯).

The musical idea accompanying the scene from *The Miraculous Mandarin* in which the Mandarin chases after Mimi (Ex. 3 (b)) could well have been derived from this or a very similar scale form, employing seven of the scale's nine pitches (Ex. 3(a)). This melody also illustrates Bartók's interest in mirrored patterns first demonstrated in the second of the Bagatelles for piano of 1908, the opening four bars being symmetrically disposed over A3, with rising and falling intervals of minor and augmented seconds. Symmetry and near-symmetry can be found on every level of the Concerto for Orchestra, and this topic will be discussed further in Chapter 6.

The First and Second Piano Concertos (1926 and 1931) mark important stages on the road to the Concerto for Orchestra. Whilst techniques derived from peasant music were still crucial to Bartók, he found himself increasingly drawn to pre-Classical formal models which he used in tandem with sonata form. Many composers working around this time were attracted to a neutral compositional style labelled 'new objectivity' (*Neue Sachlichkeit*) by Hindemith, which drew, among other influences, on such characteristics of Baroque music as the use of contrapuntal procedures and ostinato-like motoric rhythms, and which avoided over-sentimentality in expression. In response to a query from Edwin von der Null about the infrequent use of counterpoint in his earlier works, Bartók noted that:

In my youth my ideal of beauty was not so much the art of Bach or of Mozart as that of Beethoven. Recently it has changed somewhat: in recent years I have considerably occupied myself with music before Bach, and I believe that traces of this are to be noticed in the Piano Concerto and the Nine Little Piano Pieces.[50]

The Baroque music which particularly interested him was that of Frescobaldi, Scarlatti, and the French clavecinists Rameau and Couperin, whose keyboard compositions he performed regularly from 1910, always on the piano.

Whilst the outer movements of the First Concerto attempt to reconcile the composer's mature style with the new-found sensitivity towards Baroque techniques, the second movement looks forward to the great Sonata for Two Pianos and Percussion of 1937, the opening and closing parts of its ternary form being saturated by the sounds of percussion instruments. This movement is related, in terms of mood and colour, to a type which has been called 'night music': an impressionistic, textural music which recalls Debussy's subtle imagery, and which was in turn to influence composers of the next generation, including Lutosławski, Messiaen and Ligeti. Bartók actually used the title 'The night's music' for the fourth movement of his suite *Out of Doors* (written just before the First Concerto), an evocation of the nocturnal sounds

13

of nature – bird calls, cricket chirps, rustling leaves and so on. In a sense the 'outer shell' of the *Elegia* of the Concerto for Orchestra is the culmination of this particularly idiosyncratic Bartókian conception.

Writing about the Second Piano Concerto in 1939 Bartók explained that:

> I wanted to produce a piece which would contrast with the first: a work which would be less bristling with difficulties for the orchestra and whose thematic material would be more pleasing. This intention explains the rather light and popular character of most of the themes of my latest concerto: a lightness that sometimes almost reminds me of one of my youthful works, the First Suite for Orchestra, Op. 3 (1905).[51]

In the intervening period between the composition of the two concertos he had composed his Third and Fourth Quartets, the two Violin Rhapsodies, and the *Cantata profana*, a magical, monumental work, which marks a loosening in the composer's style, being much less abrasive and dissonant. This change was discussed by Bartók in a newspaper interview in 1938:

> All efforts ought to be directed at the present time to the search for that which we will call 'inspired simplicity'. The greater the number of those who will dedicate themselves to that, the more will disarray be avoided. – The reason why we have in the last twenty-five years attained the greatest confusion from the creative point of view is that very few composers concentrated their efforts toward this goal, and also because musical creation has relied too much on the unique value of the most unexpected and sometimes least appropriate means of expression to convey the inventive idea.[52]

The Second Concerto contains many of the same influences as the First Concerto: melodic contours derived from his Arab music studies; rhythmic motifs from Romania; elements of Baroque ritornello form, particularly the 'framework theme' which articulates the finale; and allusions to Stravinsky. Perhaps the most interesting formal feature of the Second Concerto is its overall shape: a five-movement structure pressed into a three-movement arch or bridge, for the inner movement has two slow sections surrounding a brilliant scherzo, and the outer movements have thematic connections. The formal concept of a series of epidermal layers surrounding a germ fascinated Bartók; he compared the form of the Fourth Quartet to that of a nut or seed with two outer shells and an inner kernel, a metaphor which, whilst appropriate given his biological interests, insufficiently indicates the dynamic nature of the structure, for as Lendvai points out, the material on the 'downward' curve of the arch is thoroughly transformed by the experience of the curvilinear ascent.[53]

Writing in the twenties about the Third String Quartet, Adorno likened the composer's progress to a spiral. From a historical perspective, perhaps a better metaphor would be Bartók's own arch form, for the Concerto for Orchestra can be seen both as a culmination of a musical development which reached its apex in the Fourth Quartet, and as a point of emotional return to the early patriotic style of *Kossuth* transformed by the artistic, social and intellectual experiences of the forty years that separated the two works.

3

Genesis and reception

The roots of the Concerto for Orchestra

In February 1939, Bartók wrote to his American piano student Dorothy Parrish:

The fatal influence of the Germans is steadily growing in Hungary, the time seems not to be far, when we shall become quite a German colony. . . . I would like best to turn my back on the whole of Europe. But where am I to go? And should I go at all before the situation becomes insupportable, or had I better wait until the chaos is complete?[1]

Bartók had visited the United States in April 1940 in order to give a series of concert performances, the first of which was with the violinist Jozséf Szigeti. During this visit plans were made for a longer stay, 'perhaps for several years',[2] but there is little evidence to suggest that he believed that this was going to be a permanent emigration. His mother, with whom he had always had a particularly close relationship, had died in December 1939, breaking the last major link to his homeland, and it seems that he felt that the preservation both of his family and of his manuscripts was more important than impotent opposition to the pro-Nazi régime in Hungary. Whilst he had been involved in a number of minor skirmishes with some elements of the Hungarian press in the years leading up to 1940, and had, with other leading composers, publicly protested against an Austrian Composers' Copyright Association questionnaire which had enquired as to its members' racial origins, there is no real sense in which he can be regarded either as a political refugee, or an escapee from racial intolerance, and his life was certainly not in danger. In a perhaps idealized estimate of a man who could brook no compromise, whether with an evil régime or 'in the rejection of all moral, mental, or artistic dishonesty',[3] Hans Heinsheimer felt that in leaving Hungary, Bartók 'risked much more than many a famous man would have risked who stayed on, took the devil's blood money, and counted – quite correctly – on the forgetfulness and forgiveness of the world'.[4]

Bartók, with his second wife Ditta Pásztory, finally arrived at New York on

29 October 1940. Over the first couple of seasons in the United States, Bartók had some limited success as a performer, with concert appearances, either solo, or with Ditta as duet pianist, in some thirty towns or cities. However, despite the best efforts of his publishers, Boosey & Hawkes, who had set up a concert agency to promote him with Heinsheimer as agent, concert engagements began to dwindle. Heinsheimer ascribes Bartók's lack of success to his uncompromising nature, which was reflected both in his choice of repertoire, which was demanding of the audience, and in his concert persona, which was stiff, cold and aloof if dignified.[5] Bartók was clearly becoming aware of his problems; writing to his son Béla in June 1941 he noted (in a tone that may bring into question his much vaunted unwillingness to compromise):

Our prospect of breaking into the concert world is not very bright: either our agent is bad, or the circumstances are not favourable (and will become even less so in the near future, as a result of wartime atmosphere). In these circumstances we should then have to return to Hungary, no matter how the situation develops there . . . if things are bad everywhere, one prefers to be at home.[6]

His career as a concert pianist finally ended in January 1943 with a performance of the Concerto for Two Pianos and Percussion,[7] conducted by Frigyes (Fritz) Reiner, with Ditta as second pianist.

In January 1941, partly as a result of the good offices of Carl Engel, the president of Schirmers, Bartók was offered a one-year bursary by Professor Douglas H. Moore of the Music Department of Columbia University from its Alice M. Ditson Fund, at an annual salary of $3000, to transcribe and analyse Serbo-Croatian folk songs from the Milman Parry collection. This collection contained some 2600 double-sided disks, and approximately 600 individual items,[8] and Bartók's work (for which the bursary was extended to a second year) involved the transcription and morphology of women's songs.[9] During this period of ethnomusicological study, he composed no new music, partly because of continuing ill-health, partly because of the intensity of the folk-song research, but mainly because of his general sense of alienation, which was exacerbated by the difficulty of the conditions he was working and living under in New York, a much noisier and more intrusive environment than Budapest.

Bartók suffered from intermittent debilitating bouts of ill-health throughout his life. In early childhood he had a painful rash which lasted through his first five years, as a student he developed tuberculosis, and, according to his son Béla, he had a serious disease every year from January to March.[10] His final summer in Hungary was marked by arthritic pains in the shoulders which made it difficult to play the piano, and this problem recurred in August 1941, whilst he was staying at Agatha Fassett's Riverton country house. In December 1942, in a letter to Wilhelmine Creel, he remarked that he had been subject to a temperature of about 100° almost every evening since the beginning of April, and that his doctors were unable to produce a diagnosis.[11] It is probably no coincidence that this prolonged period of ill-health occurred when his financial situation was at a particularly low ebb. During the spring of 1943 his condition deteriorated, and he became convinced that he would never appear in public again. Heinsheimer was instructed to cancel any forthcoming lectures, and to take no further bookings for recitals.

His weight having fallen to only 87 pounds,[12] he finally collapsed in February 1943, after delivering the third of a series of lectures about the '"New" Hungarian art music' at Harvard University,[13] and he was taken to hospital from his home. Doctors were unable to produce any positive diagnosis of his condition during the few days he stayed under observation (his immediate medical fees having been paid by Harvard University), and it was suggested that he should undergo further tests with the pulmonary specialist, Dr Oppenheimer, at Mount Sinai Hospital, the expenses again being covered by Harvard.[14] Oppenheimer believed that Bartók's problems were associated with tuberculous lesions,[15] and sent him home with a poor prognosis, expecting him to live for only a few weeks.

Ditta now felt obliged to contact her husband's friends and admirers and ask for assistance, which came in the form of a number of donations of small sums of money. Meanwhile Ernő Balogh, one of Bartók's earliest piano pupils, contacted ASCAP (the American Society of Composers, Authors and Publishers, the sister organization to the British Performing Right Society of which Bartók was a member). ASCAP responded by offering assistance to cover the composer's further medical expenses, much to Bartók's irritation.[16] With ASCAP's financial support, Bartók was hospitalized again, this time at the Doctor's Hospital, under the supervision of the Hungarian expatriate Dr Israel Rappaport. During his seven-week stay, from mid-March to the beginning of May, the diagnosis was reassessed, and his condition was determined to be chronic myeloid leukaemia, a disease of the blood in which the white-cell population increases dramatically, and which produces symptoms including the loss of weight, pain in the upper-left abdomen, and in some cases a hypermetabolic state resulting in sweating.[17] Bartók was never informed of this diagnosis, but was told much later, probably as a placebo, that he was suffering from polycythemia, a disease which had a better prognosis than leukaemia, and which, ironically, is characterized by an increase in the red-blood-cell population.[18]

At the same time, Reiner, and Bartók's longtime friend, the violinist József Szigeti, approached the conductor Serge Koussevitzky, suggesting that he should commission a new orchestral work from the sick and disheartened composer. The American-naturalized Russian Koussevitzky, who had married the daughter of a Russian tea millionaire in 1905, had taken over the baton of the Boston Symphony Orchestra in 1924 and transformed it from mediocrity to one of the country's finest ensembles. He was familiar with some of Bartók's music, having conducted, among other things, the first performance of the orchestral version of *Village Scenes* in 1927, and the First Piano Concerto. On the death of his wife Natalie he established the *Koussevitzky Music Foundation* in her memory. It was from this fund that a commission was to be given to Bartók, in the expectation that he would probably be too ill to complete a new work, but that the fee would provide some assistance in his final days. In Koussevitzky's letter, dated 4 May 1943, offering the grant of $1000 in two instalments ('$500 on receipt of the acceptance, and $500 upon the completion of the manuscript'), he stipulates that the work should be for orchestra and dedicated to the memory of Natalie Koussevitzky. In his final paragraph, he remarks that he is looking forward 'to an opportunity to talk this matter over with you in the near future'.[19]

Writing a letter of thanks for his assistance to Szigeti on 23 May 1943, Ditta mentions Koussevitzky's visit to her husband in his hospital ward:

They agreed on a purely orchestral work; it was Béla's idea to combine chorus and orchestra. I am so glad that plans, musical ambitions, compositions are stirring in Béla's mind – a new hope, discovered in this way quite by chance, as it were incidentally.

One thing is sure: Béla's 'under no circumstances will I ever write any new work - - -' attitude has gone. It's more than three years now - - -[20]

Heinsheimer decorates his description of the meeting between composer and conductor with a little conceit, likening it to the commissioning of Mozart's Requiem:

The conductor was alone. He took a chair, moved it close to the bed, and began to explain his mission. He had come to offer Béla Bartók a commission from the Koussevitzky Foundation – a commission carrying one thousand dollars – and the assurance of a first performance by the Boston Symphony Orchestra. The composer was free to choose any form of music he cared to write. There was just one condition: the score was to be dedicated to the memory of Mrs Natalie Koussevitzky, the conductor's wife, who had died a few years earlier and in whose memory the foundation had been established. It was to be a requiem after all![21]

It seems that Bartók had considerable qualms about accepting money for a commission that he might not be able to complete and had to be persuaded by Koussevitzky that the foundation, once it had made its decision, was obliged to pay the composer, whether or not the commissioned work was finished.[22]

On the day following Koussevitzky's visit, Bartók returned home in a state of great animation, apparently transformed in his state of mind, if not of health. A month later, in order to convalesce, he was moved to a private sanatorium at Saranac Lake in the Adirondack Mountains in the north of New York State, accompanied by Ditta and his youngest son Péter, staying from 1 July until 12 October, the fees again being paid by ASCAP. It was during this stay, from 15 August until 8 October, at the start of a sustained period of remission from the effects of leukaemia, that the Concerto for Orchestra was composed.[23]

The concept of a Concerto for Orchestra

From the mid-1920s a number of orchestral works bearing the title Concerto but without soloists began to appear, many of which were modelled on the Baroque concerto grosso, or at least a reinterpretation of it. The essential features of this prototype include the suppression of individual virtuosity by the use of a *concertino* group of soloists, the size and disposition of which can be subject to change in the course of the work, and the use of an architecture articulated by a repeating ritornello structure generally performed by the full ensemble. As a musical framework, it is often less concerned with tonal polarization and thematic development than sonata form is, and, unlike the heroic, hyper-expressive nineteenth-century solo concerto, is apparently driven by consensus and compromise rather than confrontation.

Works composed in this neoclassical genre include Hindemith's four-movement Concerto for Orchestra Op. 38 of 1925 (which employs a regular ritornello framework in its first movement, with a fixed *concertino* group of oboe, bassoon and violin), Roussel's three-movement Concerto for Small Orchestra Op. 24 of the same year, and Stravinsky's Concerto in E♭ 'Dumbarton Oaks' of 1938. When Bartók's publisher Ralph Hawkes wrote to him in 1942 suggesting that he might be interested in composing 'a series of concertos for solo instrument or instruments and string orchestra . . . or combinations of solo instruments and string orchestra',[24] he was probably thinking of this class of pieces, and particularly, perhaps, the Stravinsky. There is no evidence to suggest that Bartók was familiar with any of these works, but it is certain that he did know Kodály's Concerto for Orchestra, for he had brought the score with him from Hungary in 1940 in order to pass it to the commissioning organization, the Chicago Philharmonic Society.[25] This single-movement work, which was premièred on 6 February 1941, falls into five main sections conforming to an ABA'B'A" pattern. The A sections (Allegro risoluto) are dominated by a brisk melody reminiscent in a rather stylized way of Hungarian peasant music, and the B sections (Largo) by a slow expressive *cantilena*. Structurally, it is a conflation of sonata, ritornello and variation forms, the opening A section acting as an exposition and development of two main thematic ideas, with A' as recapitulation, and A" as a brief coda. There is no clearly differentiated *concertino* group employed in the work, instead many members of the orchestra are given brief opportunities to behave soloistically.

In Bartók's explanation of his Concerto for Orchestra,[26] he describes it as a 'symphony-like' work, stressing its 'tendency to treat the single instruments or instrument groups in a "*concertant*" or soloistic manner', a form of behaviour it has in common with Kodály's. Although it shares its nomenclature with other neoclassical orchestral concertos, and displays allusions to a ritornello framework in its first movement, it is also possible to locate it in the tradition of the nineteenth-century symphony. Indeed, Adorno remarks that Bartók's late works are not returns to defunct forms of expression, but 'represent an almost naïve continuation of the Brahms tradition'.[27] Bartók had previously composed only a single work bearing the title symphony, a piece which he had soon suppressed, namely the immature Symphony in E♭ of 1902, which bears the influence of both Strauss and the *verbunkos* style of Hungarian gypsy music. All of his other orchestral works up to the Music for Strings, Percussion and Celesta of 1936 (including the Four Orchestral Pieces of 1912,[28] which comes closest to a symphonic plan) are suite-like rather than symphonic in their organization. The Concerto for Orchestra can thus perhaps be seen as the symphony which had previously either eluded him, or which he had self-consciously avoided, bringing his life's work full circle in a piece which utilizes elements of both the *verbunkos* and peasant musics in the mature Bartókian style.

At the time of composition of the Concerto a five-movement plan was relatively unusual in the symphonic repertoire, the most familiar examples being Beethoven's Sixth, Berlioz's *Symphonie fantastique*, Schumann's Third, and Mahler's Second, Fifth and Seventh Symphonies. Of these works, it is probably Mahler's Seventh Symphony of 1906, with its pairing of serenades (*Nachtmusik*) as second and fourth movements, which comes closest to a Bartókian conception of form, although Bartók seems to have had little sympathy for Mahler, describing his music in 1937, along with that of

Bruckner and Strauss, as 'congested and bombastic'.[29] He had already explored five-movement formats in his First Suite for Orchestra (a work for which he retained a fondness throughout his life), the *Hungarian Sketches*, the suite for piano *Out of Doors*, the Second Piano Concerto,[30] and the Fourth and Fifth String Quartets. The three latter pieces employ relatively symmetrical structures in which the outer movements (one and five, two and four) are variants of each other, the overall shape of the works being kinds of arch or bridge. Such a method of construction is seen explicitly in the first and third movements of the Concerto for Orchestra, and in a rather more general way, in the work as a whole.

The composition of the Concerto

Writing to his former piano student Wilhelmine Creel on 17 August 1943 from Saranac Lake, Bartók gives no indication that he has started to compose the Concerto, but tells her that he is killing time by reading, most recently, an early translation of Don Quixote.[31] It seems, however, that he had begun the work just two days earlier, working remarkably rapidly given his state of health. Six weeks later, on 26 September, he indicates to his son Péter that the work is progressing well:

I am working on the commissioned piece. I do not know whether there is any connection between this and the improvement in my health, but in any case I am very busy. Practically most of the day is taken up with it. It is a long work: 5 movements. But the first 4 are already finished. Now I am having trouble with the last, which for certain reasons is the most difficult. In a thing like this there is always a lot of petty detail, although far less than writing a scientific work. I would like to be able to finish it here.[32]

The finale took a further fortnight to compose, and the work was completed, fully orchestrated, on 8 October 1943, just fifty-four days after it was begun. It is scored for triple woodwind (with doublings on piccolo, cor anglais, bass clarinet and double bassoon), four horns, three trumpets, three trombones and tuba, timpani, percussion,[33] two harps and strings.

Bartók's compositional processes when writing orchestral works varied somewhat throughout his career, but they generally consisted of a chain of events beginning with sketches which were expanded into a continuity draft, usually, in the case of the orchestral works, in the form of a *particella* or short score, and then orchestrated in a final copy.[34] Later stages in the chain included the manufacture of further copies with revisions, either by the immediate family or by professional copyists; the correction of proofs; and the printing of a final authorized edition. The sketches for the Concerto for Orchestra are to be found in the second of a series of three 'pocket-books' of sketches and transcriptions.[35] This second pocket-book also includes transcriptions of Turkish music dating from his 1936 folk-song collecting trip to Anatolia. Unusually, the sketches and the continuity draft are merged, the former written in pen, the latter (in the form of a *particella*) in pencil, with fairly detailed indications of the orchestration. Exceptionally for works written by Bartók after 1929, the final score is written on manuscript paper (Belwin Inc. Parchment Brand, No. 19, 24 stave) rather than the transparent paper which he normally used to simplify the publisher's lithographic process.

The manuscript is a fascinating record of the composer's physical and mental state; it is written with a positive, confident hand which betrays little of his weakness, and is in most respects identical to the final printed version which was revised for engraving by Erwin Stein (who like Heinsheimer had formerly worked for Universal Edition).[36] On the title page Bartók describes the work as 'Concerto per Orchestra', and on the verso he provides a complete list of timings for all the sections of the piece, an idiosyncratic feature of his later scores which has encouraged some dubious analytic approaches, in particular the use of the golden section by Lendvai and his followers. A small number of errors appeared in the first printed edition (all of which have been corrected in the 1993 reprint), most notably the misreading of the metronome mark for the second movement as $\text{\textquoteright}=74$ instead of the intended $\text{\textquoteright}=94$.[37] Interestingly, the second movement was originally entitled 'Presentando le coppie' instead of the now familiar 'Giuoco delle coppie'.[38] According to the composer's friend Antál Doráti, this second title was the result of discussion among Bartók's circle of acquaintances:

'How would you say in Italian "Páros Gemutató"?' – he asked us. The literal English translation of these Hungarian words would be: 'Pair-wise presentation'. This, of course, would be a precise title for that movement. But we could not translate it into any other language, in any way that was both accurate and usable. So, after much discussion, we agreed upon 'gioco della [*sic*] coppie', 'game of couples' – an incorrect title, because it stresses the game element, which the music does not, and can thus lead to misinterpretation.[39]

Early performance history

The world première of the Concerto was given to a full auditorium of subscribers at a matinée concert in Symphony Hall Boston on Friday 1 December 1944 at 2.30 p.m., by the Boston Symphony Orchestra conducted by Koussevitzky, the programme being repeated on the following evening.[40] The first half of the concert consisted of Mozart's Overture *Idomeneo* and Franck's D minor Symphony, the second of the Bartók.[41] The composer, rather against his doctor's better judgement, attended the rehearsals and the première, and was extremely satisfied:

> . . . the performance was excellent. Koussevitzky is very enthusiastic about the piece and says it is 'the best orchestra piece of the last 25 years' (including the works of his idol Shostakovich!). At least this is his personal opinion - - - .[42]

According to Agatha Fassett, he felt that 'no composer could have hoped for a greater performance',[43] though a review by Rudolph Elie in the *Boston Herald* of a second pair of performances on 29–30 December suggests that there were some rough edges in the première which 'created a certain tension or excitement' and added to the general brilliance of the occasion. The audience appears to have responded warmly to this new work of a composer who still had something of a reputation as a dangerous modernist to American concertgoers. As Elie, a supporter of Bartók's music, suggests in a piece for the *Herald* of 3 December 1944 headlined 'The People vs. Bartók: is there really a case?' (Appendix (b)), even those who could accept the music of Schoenberg and Krenek found Bartók's extremely difficult. After the performance he was 'most cordially received when Dr Koussevitzky escorted him to the platform', and he 'bowed with grave shyness'.[44]

The Boston Symphony Orchestra records indicate that after a cluster of performances in 1944–5 (1–2 and 29–30 December 1944, and the New York première 10 and 13 January 1945), all conducted by Koussevitzky, the work lay unplayed by that ensemble until 1950 when it received three performances under Richard Burgin. During the fifties it was performed on another dozen occasions under Ansermet, Burgin, Monteux and Doráti. By the sixties the work had become a more regular feature of the orchestra's repertoire, being performed under the baton of Leinsdorf some twenty-six times throughout the United States and Canada.

The Boosey & Hawkes hire-library ledger evinces the work to have been performed on some seventy-two occasions throughout Europe in the period up to 1950. The first performance outside Britain and the United States was given in Brussels, by the Société Philharmonique de Bruxelles, on 18 January 1946. The London première was given by Boult and the BBC Symphony Orchestra on 6 March 1946, and repeated four days later. It was performed on some ten subsequent occasions in England by professional ensembles in the four-year period, mainly by the BBC. The Hungarian première appears not to have taken place until 5 January 1948, though the hire record is ambiguous, giving the forwarding date for the parts as 20 December 1947, the performance date as 5 January 1947 [*sic*], and the return date as 4 March 1948. It appears to have received only one further performance in Hungary before 1950, though given political difficulties, unreported concerts may possibly have taken place.

In 1944 Bartók produced a piano reduction of the score which was intended to be used for a ballet. According to Doráti, whose connections with the ballet world had encouraged Heinsheimer to use him as an intermediary, he was successful in arranging for the American Ballet Company to buy an option for the stage rights, and the work went into rehearsal, choreographed by Anthony Tudor. For reasons that Doráti is unable to explain, the project was later abandoned.[45] It seems that Doráti produced a recording of the Concerto for Tudor's use, and that copies were also given to Koussevitzky, on his request, to aid the preparation of the orchestral performance.

Shortly after the New York première, in February or March 1945, in response to a request from Koussevitzky, Bartók produced a second ending to the finale, some nineteen bars longer than the first. It is this second version which is now preferred. Bartók died before the score was printed by Boosey & Hawkes; final checking of engraving proofs was undertaken by György Sándor at the composer's request, probably with reference to a list of errors which has been found among Bartók's papers. Bartók also produced a document entitled *Some Additional Improvements to 'Concerto for Orchestra'*, and the suggestions contained within this have been incorporated into the 1993 revised edition.[46]

Critical reception

The reviews of the première of the Concerto in the Boston papers were unanimous in their approval of the new work. Elie was immediately convinced that this was one of Bartók's most important pieces:

It is hardly necessary at this point to remark on the strength of the musical personality disclosed by Bartok's music. His Orchestral Concerto, given yesterday for the first time, is a work which must rank as the composer's masterpiece, which is to say it must also rank among the musical masterpieces of recent years.

Despite its basic simplicity, it is a composition of great contemporary complexity and, for the most part, of typical Bartokian austerity and severity, and it was not (barring the graceful, exquisite intermezzo) taken to heart by yesterday's audience. This should not dismay Bartok, whose music has withheld its innermost secrets from the general public for years. And it is by no means clear, even today that his day is coming, but I would hazard a guess that if this extraordinary composition were to be heard as often as Shostakovitch's antiquated sensations, it would speak powerfully to the musical public.

. . . Yes, if a composition of transcendent musical art may be defined as one which, in its own way, is a summation of all that has gone before then the Orchestra Concerto is a work of art . . . and a great one.[47]

In an article printed in the *Monitor* on the day before the première, Winthrop P. Tryon had suggested that the work could best be seen as a symphony rather than a concerto, a theme he developed in a review following the matinée performance on 29 December 1944:

Now it can hardly be disputed that the Bartók Concerto . . . and the Brahms Symphony . . . belong to the same category of artistic creation. They are both orchestrated cycles in four-movement form. The Concerto, true enough, runs on a five-movement design, but the third movement and the fourth, designated Elegy and Intermezzo, are practically one on the so-called 'slow' order. These external differences are of no consequence whatever. What makes the Concerto a novelty in form and structure is the handling of the melodies and the distribution of the moods. As for a Bartók melody, it is by no means the same thing as a Brahms theme, which is subjected to elaborate and patterned development. Nor is it allowed to dominate the situation longer than enough to convey a certain feeling, perhaps joyous, perhaps sad, or perhaps ruminative.[48]

Notwithstanding the positive tone adopted through all these early reviews, it seems that the public was not completely won over by Bartók's music. According to Elie's review 'even two hearings were not enough to convince yesterday's audience that Bartok has the slightest interest in diverting or reaching it through sensuous sounds and long-flowing melodies',[49] which may help explain the five-year hiatus before the work's installation into the orchestra's regular repertoire.

Olin Downes's review of the New York première on Wednesday 10 January 1945 took up the question of Bartók's artistic integrity.[50] Rather than seeing the musical simplification which is apparent in the Concerto as a token of compromise, he believed it was indicative of the composer's courage in seeking new means of expression:

the score is by no means the nut to crack that other of Bartók's late works have offered. It is a wide departure from its author's harsher and more cerebral style. There might even be the suspicion with an artist of less sincerity than this one, that he had adopted a simpler and more melodic manner with the intention of an appeal to a wider public.

But that would not be Mr Bartók's motive. Nor would the emotional sequence of this music, and the care with which it has evidently been fashioned, support such an assumption. What is evident is the courage, which this composer never has lacked, with which he is striking out, in his late years, in new directions. The style is less involved and ingrowing than we have thought much of Bartók's late music to be, and it escapes in a large measure, the pale cast of isolated thought which has brooded over so many of his pages.

In sum, as he himself has stated, it is an emergence from the pessimism which might pardonably have engulfed him, as it has so many leading artists of today, especially those of European schools. And of all things courage is the most praiseworthy.

The Concerto was given its British première by the Liverpool Philharmonic Orchestra on 20 October 1945 in Liverpool,[51] conducted by Malcolm Sargent. The review by 'F. B.' in the *Musical Times* stressed the popular and anti-intellectual character of the work:

It had a great reception in Liverpool and will have an equally warm welcome wherever it is played for the excellent reason that in spite of subtleties of rhythm, harmony and scoring it is perfectly straightforward, offers no difficulty to any unbiased listener no matter how great his ignorance of musical theory, and is immensely cheerful. It embodies no philosophy; it has enough dissonance to make us aware that we are living in the middle of the twentieth century and no more. . . . The apparently episodical nature of the work may prove to have been due to imperfect grasp of what was happening, but the most important thing about the Concerto is that whether you know all there is to be known about the art of music or are simply looking upon music as a substitute for an after-dinner cigar (it is much cheaper than cigars at present) you cannot help being exhilarated by this kaleidoscope where nothing lasts except the vitality and ingenuity of the genial and learned showman.[52]

That the Concerto should be selected as the final work of the ISCM (International Society for Contemporary Music) Festival in London on 14 July 1946,[53] the year after his death, was a measure of the respect in which Bartók was held by the modernist community. It soon became clear, however, that the compositions of Bartók's later years, and in particular the Concerto, were seen by some musicians, especially the supporters of the Second Viennese School, to represent an artistic and musical compromise. One of the chief advocates of this view was René Leibowitz, whose polemical article 'Béla Bartók ou la possibilité du compromis dans la musique contemporaine',[54] written just two years after the composer's death, argued that the composer had reached his authentic style in the two Violin Sonatas, and particularly in the Fourth String Quartet. He found the sonatas to be 'penetrated by a real radicalism with respect to the majority of the problems of contemporary polyphony, which confers to these works a prime position at the heart of musical production during the last thirty years'.[55] The Fourth Quartet was, he felt, the true apex of Bartók's compositional output, a work which again exhibited novel solutions to the problem of polyphony, and had a clarity of which, paradoxically, the composer did not seem to be aware. For Leibowitz, Bartók had two options: to follow the path indicated by the Fourth Quartet and to work out its atonal implications; or to remain 'free', and fall into a musical style characterized by compromise. Unfortunately, as far as Leibowitz was concerned, Bartók chose the latter.

The 1946 ISCM Festival was, for Leibowitz, indicative of a general 'slide towards compromise', and the Bartók Concerto for Orchestra exemplified this in a number of ways:

the continual symmetry of phrases and periods; the stereotyped use of the superim-position by contrary motion of the same motif from a tonal centre (first movement); the parallel motion of a similar melody for two instruments always following a single vertical interval without the change of interval affecting the rest of the harmony (second movement); the 'decorative use' of a popular melody without functional relationship to the rest of the thematic material (fourth movement); and generally a loss of real harmonic control, or rather, a chaotic harmonic structure which ignores for most of the time the recent developments in this domain.[56]

Adorno's 1940s view of Bartók's music was congruent with that of Leibowitz, especially with regard to the Violin Sonatas and middle pair of Quartets. He saw it as an attempt to 'reconcile Schoenberg and Stravinsky',[57] though believed that it generally surpassed Stravinsky in terms of richness and density. He admired the music's 'extra-terrestrial' quality which gave it the potential to alienate its audience, separating it from crude nationalistic music, and aligning it with the avant-garde. By the mid-1950s, his judgement of the later pieces, as expressed in 'Modern music is growing old', was that they were:

certainly late-flowering and posthumous masterpieces; but they have been domesti-cated and contain nothing of a volcanic, savage or menacing nature. And this evolution in Bartók has a strange retroactive effect: thus, in some of his earlier works, even the most 'advanced' such as the first Violin Sonata, the music, looking back on it, seems much more innocent; what used to seem like a sort of conflagration now sounds like a sort of czardas.[58]

Analytic approaches to Bartók's music

Bartók's music has been the subject of a number of disparate analytic approaches whose methods could be very loosely categorized as idealist, materialist and empiricist: the term idealist implying some kind of external, transcendent frame of reference (here 'nature'); materialist suggesting a reliance on internal features of the music or more abstract models; and empiricist suggesting an approach which relates certain characteristics of the music to possible external influences (generally folk-music sources). There is, of course, a very wide area of overlap between these approaches, and the terms are not intended to suggest clean-cut divisions between them. This brief introduction is intended to provide a context for the discussions of the following three chapters.

Ernő Lendvai, a Hungarian scholar whose writings have been widely disseminated in the English language, is the leading exponent of the 'idealist' tendency. He has proposed a naturalist basis for many of the components of Bartók's musical language which parallels the composer's oft-quoted belief in peasant music as a natural phenomenon. For Lendvai, Bartók (and Kodály) achieved 'the *organic synthesis* of the music of East and West',[59] a characteristically sweeping statement which implies through its invocation of organicism, an imitation of the natural world, a living quality; by the use of the term 'synthesis', a reconciliation of opposites; by reference to Orient and Occident, a binary opposition between two cultures. Lendvai's concept of 'East and West' is particularly problematic, for the 'East' would seem to include Hungary, Romania, Bulgaria, Slovakia, Yugoslavia, Turkey and North Africa, territories which far exceed conventional definitions of the Orient. In a sense, what Lendvai means by the East is what lies outside western European and North American high culture, what is 'other'. For Lendvai, then, Bartók's music is a pan-cultural, supra-national, utopian art-form, which transcends the influences of its sources.

Lendvai has proposed several concepts which he believes to lie at the heart of Bartók's musical language. Of these, the most influential have been the axis system and the Fibonacci series/golden section models. The axis system is concerned with harmonic and tonal substitution; traditionally, in a diatonic context, certain chords have been able to act as substitutes for others; for example, the submediant chord (e.g. A minor in the key of C major) can replace the tonic, most familiarly in an interrupted cadence. Lendvai extends this to encompass the flat mediant (e.g. E♭ in C) which conventionally relates the tonic minor to its relative major, and more contentiously to the sharpened subdominant/flattened dominant (G♭/F♯ in C), normally regarded as the most remote pitch/chord/key area from the tonic. He then assembles three 'axes' of substitutable key areas: a tonic axis (which 'in' C would contain the pitches C–E♭–F♯–A); a subdominant one (F–A♭–B–D); and a dominant one (G–B♭–C♯–E). Within each axis are two branches: a primary one which connects the 'tonic' pole to its closest replacement (counterpole) which lies an augmented fourth/diminished fifth above (C–F♯), and a secondary one which links the other pair. The axis system, therefore, attempts to 'explain' Bartók's chromaticism within a tonally functional model.

The use of the Fibonacci series and the golden section principle form central props in Lendvai's theoretical writings, and have attracted the attention of a number of other theoreticians. The Fibonacci series is a number series derived from a recursive formula in which each subsequent element is the sum of the previous two (1, 1, 2, 3, 5, 8, 13, 21 etc.), and has the property that the ratio between neighbouring pairs of numbers increasingly approximates the so-called 'golden mean' ($\approx 0.618033..$), the accuracy increasing the further one progresses up the number series. The golden mean or *proportio divina* can be understood as the point on a line which divides it into two segments (X and Y) such that the ratio between the segments (X:Y) is the same as that between the longer segment and the entire line (X+Y:X) (see Fig. 1).

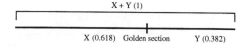

Fig. 1   The golden section ratio

Some natural forms have been shown to contain golden section proportions, at least ideally, and Lendvai and his followers have spent a considerable amount of energy identifying such points (often multiply nested) in the durational and rhythmic parameters of Bartók's music, working on the dual assumptions that the concept of a ratio in the time domain is similar to one in space, and that we hear and listen 'linearly'. We are left to draw the conclusion, it seems, that if the music is endowed, whether consciously or unconsciously, with the same ratios that nature occasionally displays, that it is thereby somehow validated by this 'link' to the natural world.

The materialist or positivist tendency is illustrated by the American scholars Elliott Antokoletz and Paul Wilson, both of whom have produced substantial theoretical studies.[60] Antokoletz is interested in symmetry in Bartók's music, not at the formal level, but in terms of the use of symmetrical horizontal and vertical (or melodic and harmonic) structures. Whilst such structures, he argues, undermine 'those properties of traditional major and minor scales that establish a sense of tonality',[61] their axes of symmetry can act as replacements

30

for tonal centres, and movement between them can function in an analogous way to modulation. He isolates three specific symmetrical 'cells' which he believes to have profound importance in Bartók's music: the X cell (e.g. C C♯ D D♯ – chromatic); the Y cell (e.g. C D E F♯ – whole tone); and the Z cell (e.g. C F F♯ B – alternating perfect fourth and minor second).

Wilson suggests that Antokoletz's approach 'seems to lead the listener or analyst past the individual musical structures of specific works, in search of a precompositional system of pitch organization that is too abstract to illuminate those individual structures'.[62] His response is to propose a hierarchical theory of pitch organization more concerned with the works as heard experiences, which he demonstrates with graphs which have something in common with those of Schenker. In Wilson's theory, points of arrival and departure – the tonics and dominants of tonal music – are not fixed before the event by abstract models, but are dynamically assigned according to their musical context (a feature which suggests that Wilson is as much an empiricist as a materialist). The graphs are intended to demonstrate that the coherence of Bartók's music is founded upon patterning at a deeper level, below the musical surface, analogous to the patterning that Schenkerian analysts observe in tonal music.

The third group of musicologists, who might loosely be called empiricists, approach the music by reference to a close study of Bartók's own folk collections, and particularly his morphological methodology. Bartók's standard practice, adapted from that of the Finnish musicologist Ilmari Krohn, is to transpose folk material so that its final pitch is G_4, pitches from the G one octave lower being labelled from I to VII, pitches from G_4 upwards being labelled from 1 to 11. The melodic structure of songs is determined by reference to the text lines of the lyrics, and the terminal pitch of each line is noted using a combination of brackets and boxes. Thus ⅃⊡⊏ represents a song whose first line ends on F_5, whose second line ends on D_5, and whose third line ends on B_4. The metric (number of syllables per line) and rhythmic structure of each line is identified, and where all lines share the same metre or rhythm they are described as isorhythmic or isometric respectively, where they have differing metres or rhythms they are called heterometric or heterorhythmic. The ambitus or range of the entire song is noted using the system of numbers indicated above, and its formal divisions marked with roman capitals – for example, A B C D indicates a four-line song, all of whose lines are different. If the structure of the piece involves a return of the opening line as the last line (e.g. A B B A) it is described as architectonic (or architectural), a characteristic of many new-style folk songs; if not, it is called

31

Ex. 4 Heterometric (8, 6, 6, 6); four-part structure: A B C Ck;
principal caesura (3); pentachord with tritone (F mode); range 1–5;
notes employed: exclusively crotchets and quavers; 2/4 'tempo giusto'[63]

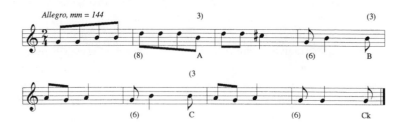

non-architectonic (a feature of old-style folk songs). Thus an entire song might be analysed as in Example 4.

Both John Downey's seminal study *La musique populaire dans l'œuvre de Béla Bartók*, and Yves Lenoir's more recent *Folklore et transcendance dans l'œuvre américaine de Béla Bartók (1940–1945)* compare the melodic, rhythmic, harmonic and formal patterns found on the surface of Bartók's music with folk sources, in particular, the structure and morphology of its melodic lines. Their interest is thus with only some of the events on the foreground of the music; they point out the fragments of peasant music set into the musical texture, but do not attempt to account for any perceived unity. Peasant music sources identified by Downey, Lenoir and others will be considered in the synopsis in Chapters 4 and 5.

The influence of the Concerto for Orchestra

Several orchestral concertos were composed and performed almost concurrently with Bartók's: the Swiss composer Gottfried von Einem's was premièred on 3 April 1944 in Berlin by the Berlin State Opera Orchestra conducted by Karajan, and the Estonian Nikolai Lopatnikoff's Concertino for Orchestra (also commissioned by Koussevitzky) was premièred by the Boston Symphony on 2 March 1945. Whilst Bartók's Concerto is clearly part of a tradition, rather than its originator, it has undoubtedly influenced a number of other composers who were not particularly interested in the concerto as neoclassical rediscovery. According to Tallián the Concerto was adopted by the Hungarian musical establishment as a model of an appropriate contemporary style for a socialist composer, in much the same way that Shostakovich's Fifth Symphony was embraced by the Soviet Union.[64]

Lutosławski's three-movement Concerto of 1954 bears the deep impression of Bartók's, particularly in its use of folk-derivative material, whilst drawing on Baroque models in the finale's conjunction of *Passacaglia, Toccata et Chorale*. Michael Tippett's 1963 Concerto is, like his Second Piano Sonata, a by-product of the opera *King Priam*; his orchestra for the first movement (of three) is divided into nine small ensembles, grouped in sets of three, each set being distinguished by specific musical characteristics, and the music concerns itself first of all with the exposition of these musical characteristics, and then with their interaction in various fashions as 'jam sessions'.[65] Elliott Carter's magnificent Concerto of 1970, which takes orchestral virtuosity to hitherto unexplored regions, has a not dissimilar premise; his orchestra is divided into four groups by range and timbre, each associated with one of the four movements of the work, which interlock and interplay with each other in an enormous cross-cutting collage.

In Roberto Gerhard's note for his own 1965 Concerto for Orchestra, he provides a perceptive consideration of the genre, which is as applicable to Bartók's Concerto and those that followed it:

The comparatively recent form of the concerto for orchestra might be said to be one in which performance is already relevant at the inception stage, since the shape and style of the piece, as well as a good deal of actual musical incident, are conditioned – sometimes fully determined – by that manner of playing we call *ensemble playing*.

Ensemble playing, the distinguishing feature of the concerto for orchestra, in fact here takes the place of the virtuoso soloist in the traditional concerto. As a result one of the composer's tasks is to provide such varied instances of virtuoso team-work as will show up the quality of the orchestra as an ensemble. Clearly, this takes us rather a long way from the formal pattern of the soloist concerto.[66]

4

Synopsis I

Overview

Bartók's tendency to demarcate the boundaries of the individual sections of his later pieces by precisely noting their durations suggests a composer who is as concerned with the juxtaposition of formal units as 'organic' organization. This concern seems to be reinforced by his own analysis of the Concerto for Orchestra, which emphasizes its block-like construction, even in the sonata forms of the first and fifth movements – a viewpoint which may seem crude to the reader schooled in Schenker's 'organic' theory of sonata form. His description of these two movements as being 'written in a more or less regular sonata form' is problematized in the first, both by the reversal of the themes in the recapitulation (producing an 'arched' structure – I II development II I – a favoured scheme of his), and because the second subject does not return in the key area of the first, and is therefore not subsumed within its tonal sphere of influence.

This is, of course, a reasonably common strategy in the late Romantic symphony – in the first movement of Brahms's F major Third Symphony, for example, the second idea appears in the mediant major (A major) in the exposition, and in the submediant major (D major) in the recapitulation. Although Lendvai's theory does clarify Brahms's tonal scheme, it does not satisfactorily explain the tonal relationships in Bartók's Concerto for Orchestra. Whereas in the first movement of the Sonata for Two Pianos and Percussion (which is effectively 'in' C) he is able to explain the key area of the second subject of the exposition (E) as a substitute dominant, and those of the recapitulation (A and F♯) as substitute tonics, no such relations hold in the Concerto.[1] Here the fundamental tonality is F, the second subject appears in the exposition 'in' B (a substitute tonic), and is recapitulated first in A (substitute dominant), then in G (substitute subdominant)! A fuller discussion of the problems of Lendvai's axis theory will be reserved for the final chapter.

Although the Concerto is fundamentally tonal, in that it has clearly defined pitch centres and makes strategic use of functional triadic harmony, it is a work whose chromaticism can frustrate attempts to view it simply as a late-flowering diatonic piece, and to label its harmonic progressions with roman numerals in the manner of William Austin.[2] This chromaticism results from the superimposition of different modes which share the same fundamental note (a method Bartók describes as 'polymodal chromaticism'):[3] it is not the result either of altering scale degrees or of the regular throughput of the twelve pitch-classes of atonal music, and it can produce passages of considerable harmonic and tonal ambiguity. Generally speaking, some caution is required when considering the tonal and formal ramifications of the work, and comparisons with earlier practice, appeals to abstract theory, or even reliance on Bartók's own writings, may sometimes confuse as much as clarify.

The overall form of the Concerto for Orchestra is as follows:

Movement	Tempo marking	Title	Tonality	Form	Duration
I	Andante non troppo	*Introduzione*			
	Allegro vivace		F	Sonata	9'47"[4]
II	Allegro scherzando	*Giuoco delle coppie*	D	Chain with trio (abcde T a'b'c'd'e')	5'57"
III	Andante, non troppo	*Elegia*	C♯	Chain with prelude and postlude (pABCp)	7'11"
IV	Allegretto	*Intermezzo interrotto*	B	ABA [int] BA	4'08"
V	Pesante–Presto	*Finale*	F	Sonata	8'52"

Whilst this scheme is not symmetrical in the sense of the Fourth and Fifth String Quartets and the Second Piano Concerto, there is certainly a significant interior 'kernel' (the *Elegia*), flanked by an inner pair of serenade- or intermezzo-like movements and an outer pair of sonata-form movements. Although the only melodic material which is literally reused between movements is that of the *Introduzione*, which reappears as the outer links in the *Elegia*'s chain structure, the work is saturated on the motivic level by themes derived from the fragment illustrated in Example 5. This melodic formula is not derived from any conventional western diatonic mode, although it is octatonic (alternating tones and semitones) as far as the B_4.[5] Such a pattern is found in both the Arab scale already discussed (Ex. 3a) starting from its third note, and in several of the Serbo-Croatian melodies that Bartók transcribed

Ex. 5   Germinal motif for the Concerto for Orchestra

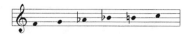

from the Milman Parry collection, including number 27c,[6] *Polećela dva vrana gavrana* (see Ex. 6).

Ex. 6   *Serbo-Croatian Folk Songs*, number 27c, bar 6[7]

In this same collection, Bartók mentions 'a very peculiar scale formation', namely F G Ab Bb Cb, which is uncommonly used and 'intermediate between the diatonic and "chromatic" scale'.[8] His final ethnomusicological foray can thus be seen to have had more than just a scientific outcome, for the folk songs and their style of performance provided him with the final ingredient in his potent mix of peasant music and high art.

First movement (*Introduzione*)

Andante non troppo 3/4 (♩=ca.73–64)

1–34	Introduction part 1 (♩=64 from bar 30)
35–50	Introduction part 2
51–75	Introduction part 3 (♩=73)

Allegro vivace 3/8 (variable) (♩.=83)

76–148	exposition of thematic group 1 [Ritornello]
149–230	exposition of thematic group 2 (tranquillo, ♩.=70)
231–71	development part 1 (♩.=83) [Ritornello]
272–312	development part 2 (tranquillo, ♩.=76–70)
313–95	development part 3 (♩.=83–90) [Ritornello]

| 396–487 | recapitulation of thematic group 2 (tranquillo, ♩.=70) |
| 488–521 | recapitulation of thematic group 1 (♩.=83) [Ritornello] |

1–34 Introduction part 1

As Bartók implies in his own programme note for the Concerto, the term 'introduction' refers to the first seventy-five bars, and not the entire first movement. The *Introduzione* can be usefully compared to the introduction to the first movement of the Sonata for Two Pianos and Percussion of 1937, which forms a similar, if shorter, structural upbeat. The opening figure, which is reminiscent of the depiction of night at the beginning of *Duke Bluebeard's Castle*, is pentatonic, rising upwards, then spiralling down through a succession of perfect fourths in the cellos and basses (see Ex. 7).

Ex. 7   Opening theme of the *Introduzione*

This melodic fragment, whose contour is related to that of the first line of the new-style Transdanubian melody *Idelátszik a temető széle* (Ex. 8),[9] bears few of the other characteristics of Hungarian folk song, other than, perhaps, its pentatonic basis and occasional ♩ ♩ rhythm.

Ex. 8   First line of the new-style Transdanubian melody *Idelátszik a temető széle* transposed to the same pitch as the opening of the Concerto[10]

The text of this song is particularly revealing, given that the Concerto was the first work to be completed after his mother's death:

> From here is seen the graveyard's border
> Where rests she who was the light of my eyes.
> The grave holds her, whom I would hold.
> Now only I know how thoroughly I am orphaned.

Ex. 9   First two phrases of the synthetic *parlando-rubato* melody

pp

Over its final note, a pedal C♯, the tremolando muted upper strings outline a symmetrical pattern, which rises through major seconds, reaching its apex on a whole-tone cluster, before returning by the pitches it had avoided on its ascent from C_5. At bars 10–11 the flutes superimpose an asymmetrical wedge-like shape which opens out and terminates on an $F\sharp_4/F_5$ dyad. The first eleven bars, whose tremulous mood prefigures the 'night music' of the third movement, form a template which is used as the basis of two sequential repetitions, though in each case the cellos and basses retain the initial C♯ and F♯,[11] and the final version is adapted and extended, ending on D♯ rather than the expected B. The first flute completes the section with an improvisatory line, which circles $C\sharp_6$ and prefigures the quasi-Hungarian melody to be unfurled in the next section.

35–50 Introduction part 2

Against a pedal E3 in the timpani, a two-bar ostinato figure using interlocking chains of perfect fourths (an extension of the opening three notes of the first section) is set up in the lower strings. The inner four notes of its first bar (A–D–C–F) anticipate the second and third bars of the first theme of the Allegro vivace (compare Ex. 11). At bar 38, this becomes a simple two-part contrapuntal texture which overlays rising and falling renditions of the ostinato in continually changing modal versions. A synthetic four-line old-style *parlando-rubato* Hungarian melody, whose final note is E, is superimposed at bar 39 by three trumpets, as if from a distance (see Ex. 9). Although this melody has a number of features in common with peasant music,[12] it does not appear to have been derived from any specific folk song, and its use of ♪♪♪♩ is uncharacteristic of old-style Hungarian music.

51–75 Introduction part 3

The pedal tone now reaches G, and the counterpoint in the lower strings dissolves to a single strand played in octaves, supported by the first and second horns sustaining the pedal and the final two notes of each phrase. Above this,

Ex. 10 Opening of the *verbunkos*-style melody

the violins, doubled by upper woodwinds, play a melody which is a variant
of the trumpet theme of the previous section, now loudly and adapted to a
verbunkos-style of performance (see Ex. 10). The tonality initially appears to
be C (the pitches of the first violins in bars 51–2 are closely related to the so-
called gypsy scale),[13] but by bar 58 it has progressed to E♭. While the violin
melody descends through the germinal pitches E♭$_7$–D$_7$–C$_7$–B$_6$–A$_6$, the lower
strings set up a new ostinato, which is basically a retrograde of this figure (E♭–
F–G–A♭–A–F♯). The rest of the woodwind gradually joins in a crescendo,
taking up the ostinato figure in an accelerating passage which forms a large-
scale upbeat to the Allegro vivace.

Allegro vivace

76–148 Exposition of thematic group 1

The assertive first idea (first and second violins) is in F, and begins with a
variant of the ostinato figure from the previous section (from which it appears
to be a logical continuation), in which the third note has been flattened, and
a pentatonic termination added (the retrograde of the final four notes of the
opening pentatonic idea of the introduction) (see Ex. 11). Whilst the outline
of the first bar of this theme is similar to that of the Serbo-Croatian melody
of Example 6, it also reveals some of the characteristics of Slovak music,
especially in its use of the interval of the tritone, and its *tempo giusto* style.[14]
Its basic shape has a family likeness to the opening theme of the Vivace section
of the first movement of the Sixth String Quartet,[15] and its irregular 3+3+2
barring is reminiscent of the *aksak*, or Bulgarian rhythm, which Bartók used
in a number of works.[16] The statement of the three-bar motif is immediately
answered by a rhyming, near inversion of it which ends on B. This opening
theme is more closely related to a classical sentence construction than any
peasant melody, and can usefully be compared to the first subjects of
Beethoven's Op. 2/1 and Op. 10/2 Piano Sonatas. Its completion, in which
black-note pentatonic elements dominate (bars 82–93), can be seen as an
example of what Schoenberg calls *liquidation* – the gradual removal of

Ex. 11   First subject

Ex. 12   Trombone extension of interlocking-fourths idea

characteristic features from a melodic line.[17] The second part of the thematic group, following a 2/8 bar rest (bar 94), is a lyrical melody played by the upper strings in a chain of open-voiced second-inversion triads – perhaps a late tribute to the influence of Debussy – and presents a more regular and lyrical foil to the previous idea, although allusions to the opening allegro figure appear as contrapuntal asides. Through this subsection, the bass part moves down from C, through B♭, to A♭, then chromatically down to E♭. The section ends with an apparently new idea in the trombone, which is based on the interlocking perfect-fourths figure of both the introduction and first subject (bars 77–8), over a pedal tremolando B♯/C♯ (see Ex. 12).

149–230 Exposition of thematic group 2

After an open fifth on C played by the first violins and cellos, the tonality settles on B (in Lendvai's theory the counterpole of, or most direct substitute for, F), and the dynamic level drops to *piano*, for the tranquil second-subject group. The almost improvisatory melodic line in the first oboe employs an extremely narrow range (at first an oscillation between just two pitches), and a rhythmic pattern derived from the second bar of the first subject (quaver, dotted quaver, semiquaver). Lenoir suggests that it is 'inspired by the scarcely

Ex. 13   Opening of second subject

modulated chants of the bards of the desert accompanied by the two-string rabab'.[18] It certainly compares strongly to the melodies called Knéja which Bartók collected in Biskra (North Africa) in 1913 (see Ex. 13).[19] The theme is repeated from bar 174 in a shortened version (the five-bar phrases are reduced to three-bar ones) by clarinets playing in octaves initially accompanied by a simple reiteration of the notes B, E and F♯ in the harp. At bar 192, flutes, oboes and upper strings play a free inversion of the 'Arab' melody in parallel triads, against which the first harp, first clarinet and bass clarinet enunciate the germinal motif (C♯–D♯–E–F♯–G–G♯); the whole passage is then repeated, transposed down a fifth. A fragment of the germinal motif (F–F♯–G♯–A) is briefly brought to the foreground by the first flute at bar 198, before a cadence on a chord of B major with an added sixth (bar 208). In preparation for the development, the lower strings intone the rhythm of the opening of the second subject, and the upper woodwinds begin a chromatic descent of near-parallel triads which works its way back down to B. Violas, cellos and basses make a final reference to the second subject, now dressed in octatonic clothing,[20] in a passage leading to the F that provides the bass for the beginning of the development.

231–71 Development part 1

Part 1 of the development can be divided into two main sections: the first from bars 231 to 248 and the second from bars 248 to 271. Having restored the dynamic level to *forte,* Bartók distorts the main allegro theme by splitting it into its two components (played by violins and trumpets), and chromatically adapting it to its new context of D♭. The D minor chord unexpectedly assembled around the trumpets' F_5 is punctuated by reiterations of the first five notes of the germinal motif transposed to D. A similar format is adopted for the consequent from bar 237, now around E♭. From bar 242 a symmetrical wedge-like shape, formed from transposed versions of the motif, surrounds a rising whole-tone scale in the horns, which ascends to C♯ before dropping back to A in bar 248, a gesture which may refer back to the passage from bars

118 to 121. The second, contrapuntal part of this section, scored mainly for strings, concerns itself with the interlocking-fourths component of the allegro theme, firstly in a two-voice canon (bars 248–54) around C/F outlining an octatonic segment (A, C, D, E♭, F, A♭), then in three-part imitation (254–7) producing a second octatonic segment (G, B♭, C, D♭, E♭, G♭), and finally in two close (dotted crotchet, then crotchet) four-voice stretti.

272–312 Development part 2

The second stage of the development, marked Tranquillo, decreases the dynamic level to *piano*. It contains three statements of a new idea related to the second subject with something of the character of the interlocking-fourths idea of the first subject. The melody, whose phrase structure is articulated in regular three-bar units (imposing a higher-level triple time), is played in A♭ by the first clarinet with a fairly light accompaniment in the upper strings, then in E by the cor anglais, and finally in a melodically reduced and rhythmically augmented version in C♯ by the bass clarinet. In bars 308–11 the flute and clarinet clearly indicate this new idea's relationship to the interlocking-fourths theme by altering it to D♭–A♭–B♭–F. The section finishes where it began, in A♭.

313–95 Development part 3

The Allegro vivace tempo and *forte* dynamic is restored with yet a new variant of the germinal figure encompassing a perfect fourth (A–B♭–C–D♭–D) which is repeated three times. Almost immediately, the second trombone takes up the theme which was presented at the end of the exposition of the first subject (Ex. 12), and clarifies the tonality as B♭. This idea now becomes the basis of a four-voice tonal fugal exposition for brass, with tutti interjections at bars 323–4 which seem to confirm the triple 'hypermetre',[21] and suggest that the first bar of the subject has an upbeat function. The tendency to operate in three-bar units is disrupted at bar 335 when the final answer (in the first trumpet) is shortened by one bar. A brief flourish of the principal idea in C at bar 340 prepares for what is effectively a counter-exposition of the fugal subject, now in inversion, and with the second note shortened in the answer and subsequent entries. This time, however, the orchestral interjections on alternate bars suggest the possibility of a duple hypermetre, the first note of the fugue subject apparently starting on a downbeat.[22] The subject is restored to B♭ at bar 363, and given out as a six-part *stretto maestrale*, new entries arriving every bar. By bar 377 the subject has been reduced to just four pitches, B♭ E♭, A♭ and D♭, as a chain of fourths variously superimposed by eight of the brass instruments, which, with the addition of the opening of the first subject at bar 386 in yet another guise, leads to a climactic tutti on a six-bar octave A♭ (a tonic substitute according to Lendvai's theory) at bar 390.

396–487 Recapitulation of thematic group 2

The A♭ at the end of the development mutates to an A minor chord in bar 396, providing the tonal level for the first recapitulation of the second subject. The bare fifths are now played by the third and fourth horns and first harp, the upper strings gently alternating between A/E and B♭/F dyads, and the first clarinet quietly intoning a slightly varied version of the Arab-inspired melody, mainly in three-bar phrases. At bar 424 the tonality shifts to G, with a more complex instrumental texture created by a 3:4:5 polyrhythm. The melody (now in four-bar phrases) is played in three parallel octaves, in a rather unusual voicing which places flutes in the top and bottom registers, and an oboe in the middle. The subsection reaches its sudden climax in bar 438 on a chord of D♯ minor, with an extraordinary strumming effect on the harp produced by the use of a wooden or metal stick near the sound-board.[23] The third part of the second-subject group recapitulation is analogous to that of the exposition, though with considerable subtle rhythmic variation. It is connected to the previous section with a perfect cadence between an altered dominant seventh on C♯ in bar 455 and an unambiguous F♯ triad in bar 456, in one of Bartók's frequent allusions to tonal practice. At bar 456, the parallel major triads shift around F♯, and from 462 they move to C, before the preparation for the recapitulation of the first subject through an accelerando from bar 476 to bar 487, which brings together a fragment of the 'Arab theme' on E and F♯, and a new version of the germinal motif (E–F♯–G♯–A–A♯). If the A♮ is ignored, all of the other pitches add up to a whole-tone structure which, at the upbeat to bar 488, is converted into a kind of dominant on C.

488–521 Recapitulation of thematic group 1

The recapitulation of the first group functions like a massive cadence to the whole movement. Its rhythm and tonality are initially adjusted to regularize it,[24] by the change of its third note to an A♮ (supported by F major triads in the trombones), and the smoothing of its third bar so that it is now in 3/8. Its completion, from bar 494, is on the contrary more irregular, being transformed by the treatment of the first three bars (494–6) to a series of sequential repetitions beginning an aurally perceived third lower each time (F, C♯, A, F♯ and D), and by the restoration of the 3/8–2/8 alternation. Against this continuous descent, the woodwinds ascend with a series of rising scale figures which lead, at bar 509, to a B♭ pedal and a polyrhythmic texture which, by its insistence on the three notes A♭, B♭ and E♭, suggests the same 'black-note' pentatonicism heard near the end of the development. The tonic is reasserted by a final iteration of the quartal brass idea which dominated the last part of the development, and a quasi-perfect cadence in F.

Second movement (*Giuoco delle coppie*)

Allegro scherzando 2/4 ($\lozenge = 94$)

1–8	Introduction	(side drum)
8–24	A	(bassoons)
25–44	B	(oboes)
45–59	C	(clarinets)
60–86	D	(flutes)
87–122	E	(trumpets)
123–64	Trio	
165–80	A'	(bassoons)
181–97	B'	(oboes and clarinets)
198–211	C'	(clarinets and flutes)
212–27	D'	(flutes and oboes)
228–52	E'	(trumpets)
252–63	Coda	(side drum, woodwind, horns and trumpets)

1–8 Introduction

Bartók's original title for the movement, 'Presentando le coppie' (pairwise presentation), perhaps better encapsulates its spirit and form than does the later 'Game of pairs',[25] for it is a chain of dances in which couples are first presented, each with their own character and voice, and then, after the

Ex. 14 Openings of the five links of the second-movement chain
showing thematic relationships

intervention of the central chorale, allowed to intermingle and adopt each others' customs and manners.[26] The side drum, (without snares), which is used as an integrating feature of the movement (appearing at the introduction; briefly at bar 32, as a preparation for and throughout the trio; and during the short coda), acts as the master of ceremonies, initiating and terminating the proceedings. It also disrupts the regularity of the 2/4 metre, its accents and upbeat figures suggesting an interchange with 3/4.

8–24 A

The first link of the 'chain' is a sixteen-bar section in D for bassoons playing *piano* in parallel (mostly minor) sixths accompanied by pizzicato strings, which has something of the character of a Yugoslavian round dance called a *kolo*.[27] Its opening three bars (8–10) outline four of the pitches of the germinal motif (Ex. 5), now transposed on to D (D–E–F–A♭), with a two-semiquaver upbeat that initiates each of the four-bar phrases derived from the side drum's opening figure. The sixteen-bar section is symmetrically divided into four phrases, each of four bars, the fourth of which is an inversion of the second. The third phrase temporarily disrupts the regularity of the events, however, by effectively switching to 3/4 (bars 17–19). Harmonically the link is extremely mobile, the four phrases cadencing on F♯ minor, F♯ major, G major and D major triads respectively.

25–44 B

The second link, which is scored for oboes playing in parallel thirds (again both minor and major), is also sixteen bars long. But its phrase structure is more complex, and it is followed by a four-bar extension in the strings. The function of this section, which initially operates in three-bar phrases without any upbeat figure, appears to be modulatory, given the gradual crescendo and continual ascent of the bass line: at first chromatic (bars 25–33), then through whole tones on its progression to G (bars 33–7), and finally back down to E. Bars 28 to 32 present a varied sequence of the opening melody now extended by two bars. A two-bar phrase pattern is maintained for the rest of the section, which after a third, varied sequential repetition, outlines a decorated, falling scale of G (mainly on the crotchet beats of bars 35–8), followed by an ascent terminating on $D\sharp_5/F\sharp_5$. These pitches form the third and fifth of a major triad on B, a formation which is underpinned by the four-bar interlude in the strings (41–4); this includes, in bar 43, a reference to the octatonic segment of the germinal figure (B–C$\sharp$–D–E–E$\sharp$).

45–59 C

In the introduction to the collection of Serbo-Croatian melodies which Bartók transcribed whilst in America, he notated a melody for two *sopels* (folk oboes) playing in roughly parallel minor sevenths.[28] This form of playing seems to be determinant of the entire second movement, but most particularly this link in the chain, in which a pair of clarinets emulate the soloists of the transcription. After a three-bar peregrination around the notes $G\sharp_4$ and $F\sharp_5$, supported by E_3 and D_4 in the second violins and violas, the clarinets begin a four-bar sequential descent through an octave which ends on an oscillation between E_4/D_5 and $G\sharp_4/F\sharp_5$, at the same harmonic level as the opening of the section, but now transformed by the addition of the pitches C and B$\flat$ in the strings, and an unambiguous whole-tone scale in the second violins (bars 55–6) preparing for the many scale figures of the next link.[29] Bartók's orchestration of this harmonically static closing section is exquisite: curious glissandi terminate on harmonics in the divided first violins,[30] and an incandescent E_7 (again a harmonic) shines through the texture like a searchlight. The lower strings' interlude is now shortened to three bars, and is dislocated by the displacement of its metric pattern by a semiquaver.

60–86 D

The fourth link, for a pair of flutes playing in parallel fifths, begins on a second-inversion triad of F♯ major, and is extended to twenty-three bars, with a four-bar postlude in the lower strings analogous to that of the previous two sections. It falls into two parts: the first (bars 60–9) cadencing unexpectedly on a black-note pentatonic chord; the second starting in C, and progressing to a climax on C♯ at bar 83. At bar 62 the flutes simultaneously play two of the three possible versions of the octatonic scale, a formation found in a number of places in the Concerto, and a completion of the model of the first five notes of the germinal motif. The brilliant concertante writing for the soloists in this section perhaps most clearly justifies the work's title as Concerto rather than Symphony.

87–122 E

Over a whole-tone texture initially founded on C, two muted trumpets play a melody in parallel major seconds, a characteristic of some of the two-part Dalmatian melodies which Bartók had heard on commercial recordings during his time in America.[31] Throughout the section, which has two main formal divisions (bars 92–101 and 102–22), and stylistic features such as tremolandi and glissandi in the multiply-divided muted strings which anticipate the 'night music' of the middle movement, the whole-tone texture shifts between the two forms of the mode to accommodate the major seconds in the trumpets,[32] in a kind of tonic–dominant oscillation. A triple hypermetre set up by the trumpets' entry is disrupted by a four-bar phrase from the end of bar 104 to bar 108. The section ends, as the entire movement began, in D, with the reappearance of the side drum, as a binding element with the trio which follows.

123–64 Trio

Brass instruments intone a five-voice chorale-like melody (see Ex. 15),[33] in imitation of an organ, the rhythmic impetus of the previous section being maintained by the side drum which plays through the fermatas. Lenoir proposes this melody to be a paraphrase of the Lutheran chorale *Nun komm, der Heiden Heiland* (Ex. 16), and notes that, according to Tibor Serly, Bartók carried a pocket score of the Bach chorales with him wherever he went.[34] Although it

Ex. 15 'Chorale' melody played by the first trumpet

Ex. 16 Chorale *Nun komm, der Heiden Heiland*
transposed to the pitch of Bartók's Trio

is by no means such a clear-cut employment of a Bach chorale as is Berg's use of *Es ist genug!* in his Violin Concerto, there are sufficient correspondences between Examples 15 and 16 in terms of metre and overall melodic shape to justify Lenoir's assertion.[35] It is uncertain, however, why Bartók, an avowed atheist, should choose to place a melody with such strong religious associations in the centre of the movement. Bartók's 'chorale' begins in B, and ends in F♯, whence horns and tuba move the tonality to B♭, over which the woodwinds repeat an upbeat figure in preparation for the reprise of the first part. Throughout the Trio the phrase rhythm is articulated in three-bar units.

165–80 A'

The reprise of the first link is little different to its exposition, other than the addition of a third bassoon playing scale and arpeggio figures in counterpoint with the original pair. It remains *piano*, and on the tonal level of D.

181–97 B'

A pair of clarinets (also in thirds) simultaneously inverts the oboes' material, which this time is prefaced by an upbeat figure. It is also slightly truncated by the excision of a couple of bars, and subtly varied, particularly in the string accompaniment which is increasingly dominated by trills and tremolandi. The modulatory character is retained, and the section terminates on a B major triad.

198–211 C'

Two flutes, at first playing softly in parallel sevenths, double the original clarinet lines, creating complex four-part voicings which are schematically supported by the violins, mainly playing fourth-chords (see, in particular, the descent from bars 199 to 205). The whole-tone harmony at the end of the equivalent section in the first part of the movement, is replaced by a chord containing the pitches B_2–$G\sharp_3$–E_4–$A\sharp_4$–D_5–$F\sharp_5$, six of the seven notes of the so-called acoustic scale transposed to E (see Ex. 2). The delicacy of the final part of the link is disrupted by the return of the string interlude, now reduced to two bars, its syncopations accented by *sforzandi*.

212–27 D'

The reprise of this link begins halfway through its course, relative to its first presentation (compare bars 212 and 70). The first oboe and clarinet share a line which joins the flutes to form a series of parallel major chords in first inversion, the tonality appearing to be F over a pedal C (timpani and cellos), and they are soon joined by the rest of the woodwind. By the end of the string interlude the tonality seems to have settled on C♯.

228–52 E'

The condensed reprise of the final link is characterized by sudden dramatic dynamic changes from *mf* to *pp*. The first part of the trumpets' theme reappears intact without the addition of extra parallel voices, coloured by the same type of oscillating whole-tone structures which characterized its first presentation. Now it is transposed a ninth higher, and accompanied by pairs of semiquavers in the divided violas which have the effect of little shudders. From bar 241, the tonality of D is gradually reasserted, the whole-tone formations being replaced by diatonic ones.

252–63 *Coda*

The finality of the movement is disrupted by the addition of the minor seventh to a sustained and reiterated D major triad, producing an irresolute D^7 chord in the woodwinds, whilst the side drum signs off.

Third movement (*Elegia*)

Andante, non troppo (♩=73–64)

1–21	'Night music' 1
22–33	Transition
34–44	Chain link 1
45–61	Transition
62–85	Chain link 2
86–100	Chain link 3
101–11	'Night music' 2
112–28	Coda

1–21 *'Night music' 1*

This impassioned and elegiac movement develops the folk-type material of the introduction to the first movement in a symmetrically organized chain structure sandwiched between a prelude and postlude. It opens with the interlocking-fourths figure in the same form as it appeared from the last beat of the third bar of the introduction to the first movement (Ex. 7), but now starting on F♯, and extended through a more chromatic variant presented as a three-voice canon, each voice starting a note higher than the previous one.[36] A pedal D, played by the timpani, harp and double basses, drops to D♭, and thence to C for the next subsection. Here (bar 10) the 'night music' proper begins. The section basically articulates one chord – C–E♭–E–G–G♯–B – which is effectively a 'coloured' C chord, and is built from a scale of alternating minor thirds and minor seconds, which Lendvai calls a 1:3 model. Over this extraordinary texture of *pianissimo* trills, tremolandi, glissandi and rapid arpeggios, which may be imagined as a depiction of the nocturnal sounds of the natural world, the first oboe intones a chant around the notes $G\sharp_5$ to B_5, which, according to Downey, shows Berber-Arab influence.[37] Whilst this

50

section is harmonically static, the highest pitch of the flute's arpeggios is continually changing. From bars 19 to 22, the music suddenly and unexpectedly settles on a unison Db6, which slides up to Eb on the last beat of bar 21.

22–33 Transition 1

The 1:3 model scale which had been played as a rapid arpeggio in the previous section is slowed down to a quaver pace, and presented canonically, first by the woodwind on C, then in a shortened version by the divided violins on Bb, and finally by the clarinets in a brief outline on Ab. The piccolo restores its register from the previous section at bar 29, in a line which suggests birdsong, and the individual woodwinds support a chord of Ab_4–B_4–Eb_5–G_5 (Ab minor with a major seventh) which is built up in the strings from top note to bottom, by accenting its initiating pitches with rapid oscillations over a major fourth, a characteristic *verbunkos* gesture. In Bartók's early music, he had associated an arpeggiated figure consisting of a rising major or minor triad with a major seventh with Stefi Geyer,[38] one of his early romantic attachments, and it may be that this elegiac falling shape is a late tribute to her.

34–44 Chain link 1

The first link of this movement's chain involves a reharmonized and reorchestrated version of the first of the 'Hungarian' melodies presented in the *Introduzione* (see Ex. 9), now in 4/4 (though changing to 3/4 at the end of the second phrase), and unambiguously in E. The melody is played loudly in octaves by violins and clarinets over a sumptuous texture of tremolo strings, harps and horn chords.[39] It is accompanied by three main elements: a series of descending scales each starting a note higher than the previous one and terminating on a pair of crotchet chords;[40] a pedal E; and a 'scotch-snap' type of *verbunkos* rhythm in the trumpets, which is a continuation of a figure initiated at the end of the first transition.

45–61 Transition 2

The second transitional passage splits into two parts. Bars 45 to 53 are concerned with a tripartite variant of the melody of the previous section articulated in two-, two- and five-bar phrases, each starting a perfect fourth higher, and accompanied by a descending figure which opens out into a three-part contrapuntal texture during the second and third phrases. Bars 54 to 61 develop ideas from the concluding section of the first transition, by superimposing three types of gesture: the piccolo's quasi-improvised interjections; a tritone F♯/C played tremolando on the bridge by the violins and violas supported by stopped horns; and a semiquaver figure which is based on the reiteration of the pitches G, G♯, A and B♭ – reminiscent of the pitches of the 'Arab' melody from the first 'night music' section – played by four solo pizzicato cellos.[41] Whilst the tonality of the section is somewhat obscure, it ends on C♯, the pitch which will finish the entire movement, and which tonally prepares the way for the next link in the chain.

62–85 Chain link 2

This section lies at the heart of both the third movement, and the entire work. It involves a new four-phrase folk-like melody with an A B C D structure, which is presented twice, and which has invited comparison with old-style melodies (see Ex. 17). Lenoir suggests that this keening chromatic melody has much in common with Transylvanian funeral songs, noting that 'the general demeanour of the melody recalls the recitative used in the laments of Maramureş, during the burial of married people'.[42] It is accompanied in its first incarnation in the violas by tremolando figures in harps and violins which continue the mood of the previous section, gradually leading to a complex chord on G♯ at bars 71–2.[43] The texture is clarified when the melody is repeated, the woodwind now playing in octaves, with tutti interjections at the end of each two-bar phrase pulling the tonality to A♭ at the movement's first climax, between bars 80 and 83. The resolution on to an A♭ major triad involves an archaic-sounding unprepared suspension and resolution (D♭–B♭–C). The link ends quietly with a brief recall of the 1:3 melodic pattern from the first transition, articulated as a four-part stretto starting on G♯.

86–100 Chain link 3

The fervent, lamenting *verbunkos* theme from part 3 of the *Introduzione* is presented in E♭ in the violins and upper woodwinds, with a counterpoint of distinct character from the rest of the orchestra, using figurations which emphasize the gypsy quality of the material and its closeness to the *lassú* style of the romantic Hungarian rhapsody. It is slightly varied from its first appearance, and climaxes after a whole-bar tremolando octave D in the violins, in an emotional outpouring from bars 93 to 99 with the descent through the

Ex. 17   Slow movement, central theme

main pitches of the germinal motif (E♭–D–C–B–A), variously decorated. In the penultimate bar, the first clarinet and first flute return to the rapid arpeggiated version of the 1:3 model which dominated the first 'night music' section.

101–11 'Night music' 2

A considerably condensed version of the first night music, briefly prefaced by the interlocking-fourths motif, draws the movement quietly towards its close. The 'Arab' oboe melody has now disappeared altogether, and the flutes and clarinets present a 1:5 model figure in place of the 1:3 model (alternating perfect fourths and minor seconds), in cadenza-like fioriture over an F/B pedal. The piccolo's fragmentary utterances fall into the silence at the end of the section.

112–28 Coda

The tonality of C♯ is finally installed in a texture which recalls Schoenberg's *klangfarbenmelodie* technique, the interlocking-fourths idea being reharmonized on each new pitch with subtly changing colours. There is a brief reminiscence of the second climax at bar 118, before the movement dissolves with considerable tonal ambiguity, the final events being a high B in the piccolo (the last recollection of its birdsong-like material), and a quasi-plagal cadence suggested by the timpani's rolled F♯ and delicate C♯.

5

Synopsis II

Fourth movement (*Intermezzo interrotto*)

Allegretto (♩ = ca.114)

1–42	A
42–76	B and A'
77–119	Interruption
119–50	B' and A"

There are two distinctly different accounts of this movement's 'meaning', both claimed to have stemmed from the composer. Doráti declares that Bartók admitted to him that 'he was caricaturing a tune from Shostakovich's Seventh Symphony . . . which was then enjoying great popularity in America, and in his view, more than it merited. "So I gave vent to my anger", he said.' Doráti continues with a 'verbal statement' from Bartók:

The melody goes on its own way when it's suddenly interrupted by a brutal band-music, which is derided, ridiculed by the orchestra. After the band has gone away, the melody resumes its waltz – only a little more sadly than before.[1]

Sándor's account, as given to Fricsay, is more interesting, in that it seems to reveal an awareness of the impotence of the artist when faced with the mindless violence of an authoritarian régime. In this reading, it is not the Shostakovich/ Lehár music which is being ridiculed by the orchestra, but culture and civilization itself by a drunken mob who sing and play a debased music:

A young lover, an idealist, brings his beloved a serenade, which, after the introduction, flows through a great viola cantilena, which is then taken over by the violins. The hidden meaning is this: the serenader personifies a nation, and the ideal to which he sings is his fatherland. This great cantilena is known throughout Hungary by every child; in fact it was made famous by a fairy-tale operetta. . . . Bartók adapted this melody to make it nobler, and sings it with the serenader from the depth of his heart.

At this moment a drunken mob comes by – with fifes, trumpets and drums – interrupting the idealist just as he's singing his most beautiful song. The brutal destroyer of this scene reveals himself to be a boot-boy [*Stiefelträger²*], a rough possessor of power, who leaves ruin and waste behind him wherever he goes; he whistles a trivial melody, a gutter-song which has considerable similarity to a Lehár melody.

Bartók subsequently told Sándor that the boot symbolizes the garrison's power, which, while one is engaged in more idealistic matters, leaves terrible trails of domination and violence in its wake. Indeed one can hear the drunk throwing up depicted by the tuba.[³] Three merciless punches from the cymbals and a blow with a rifle-butt – all is quiet.

The spectre of power is gone, and the poor serenader attempts to continue his song with his broken instrument; he starts, but doesn't get beyond the introduction; again he starts his song, but only gets a little way when three little piccolo notes interrupt his voice like falling tears, ending this wonderful movement.[4]

Whichever reading better represents the movement's signification, the interruption has remained the most contentious part of the Concerto, and at least one early commentator suggested that the work would lose nothing if the entire movement was omitted. The 'impurity' of the almost Mahlerian gesture is, however, an important feature of the work, providing a rare programmatic reference in Bartók's works.

1–42 A

A three-bar introduction outlines the pitches B_4–$A\sharp_4$–E_4–$F\sharp_4$, the outer four notes of the germinal motif, about which the first melody of the movement is fixated, and a chromatic inflection of the third to sixth pitches of the *Introduzione*. The section has an overall aa'ba" structure, each of the a components being variants of a four-phrase, metrically irregular, folk-song influenced melody. Lenoir regards this as a particularly interesting example of Bartók's syncretism, for 'through the bias of a synthetic language, the composer brings together and condenses a great number of popular influences which are neutralised and dissolved in a universal folklore'.[5] Because of the melody's metrical irregularity, and insistence upon the interval of the tritone, Downey compares it to Slovak peasant music, and in particular the second of Bartók's Four Slovak Popular Songs.[6] The mode from which its pitches are derived (B, C♯, E, F♯, A♯) is somewhat unusual: if its fifth note were an A♮, it would be a pentatonic scale, but as it stands it is an entirely artificial scale form.[7] In each of its three occurrences in this section, the a melody is accompanied by what amounts to an $F\sharp^7$ chord, which is at times made explicit, and at others, merely implied. Only on its final three notes does this dominant-

Ex. 18(a)   Opening of the cantabile theme in the violin version (bars 50–4)

Ex. 18(b)   Vincze, 'Szép vagy, gyönyörű vagy Magyarország',
first line transposed to C minor

type chord resolve on to B, the melody's (and the movement's) tonic. On its second occurrence, at bar 12, the melody (in an exquisite orchestration which has the flute and clarinet in octaves, the flute taking the lower voice) is counterpointed by its approximate inversion in the bassoon. The third subsection (bars 20–32) has a modulatory feel, its melodic lines being derived from varied and inverted fragments of a, and the fourth is a simple restatement of a with a flute descant.

42–76 B and A'

It has been suggested that the opening of the cantabile melody played twice in this section (first by violas accompanied by harps and timpani, then by cor anglais and first violins supported by harps and strings) is a paraphrase of the aria 'Szép vagy, gyönyörű vagy Magyarország' ('You are lovely, you are beautiful, Hungary') from Zsigmond Vincze's 1926 fairytale operetta *A hamburgi menyasszony* (Ex. 18). According to Lenoir this melody was extremely popular between the wars and was widely known, both in the towns and the countryside.[8] If the outer shell of the movement (section A) can be regarded as a kind of rural 'folk' serenade, this melody is clearly urban in shape. Bartók's harmonization is unusual in that it initially involves a progression through part of a cycle of fifths (G^7–C minor–F–B♭[7]–E♭ aug–A♭).[9] Such progressions, which have particularly strong tonal resonances, are occasionally found in Bartók's music (for instance from bar 160 of the development section of the first movement of the Second Piano Concerto, in the slow movement of the Second Violin Concerto, and at various points in

Ex. 19(a) Opening of the Shostakovich/Lehár parody theme

Ex. 19(b) Opening of the third subject of the first movement of Shostakovich's Seventh Symphony

Ex. 19(c) Opening of the aria 'Da geh' ich zu Maxim' from *Die lustige Witwe* (The Merry Widow) transposed to E♭ major for ease of comparison

the *Divertimento*), and Lendvai suggests that their function is to 'express a kind of motion', for they generally follow harmonically static sections.[10] Despite the apparent 'C minor' tonality of the first phrase this part of the section cadences on G, and the entire section concludes with a brief repetition of the 'folk' melody from section A played quietly without a repeat.

77–119 Interruption

The interruption fractures the movement by interpolating a section which appears to be musically incongruous. Bars 69–74 present a figure based on two falling perfect fourths and a rising major second, the inversion of the first four pitches of the *Introduzione*. A three-bar passage, from bars 75 to 77, has a transitional role, maintaining the rhythmical irregularity of the previous section by utilizing a 3+2+3 quaver division of the 4/4 bar, whilst setting up a tonic–dominant vamp in E♭, over which the first clarinet begins to play a melody which burlesques both the march theme from Shostakovich's Seventh Symphony (*Leningrad*),[11] and the aria 'Da geh' ich zu Maxim' from the Hungarian operetta composer Lehár's *Die lustige Witwe* (The Merry Widow) (Ex. 19).[12]

This new idea is a rough inversion of the linear rise of the first six notes of the cantabile theme B, ensuring an element of thematic coherence within the movement, despite the musical disruption. The strange 'fairground' orchestration of bars 92–103 is very carefully handled, and is considerably subtler than might be envisaged for such an effect.

119–150 B′ and A″

After the cantabile melody is restated in muted strings (without repetition), a varied and much abbreviated reprise of section A appears, now largely dependent upon the material from bars 20 to 32. It is interrupted by a brief, otherworldly, birdsong-like cadenza for solo flute, hovering around $C\sharp_5$ and $F\sharp_5$, and supported by a chord of $D\sharp_3–A\sharp_3–D\sharp_4–G\sharp_4$, the combined effect being a pentatonic formation. The final eight bars involve the inversion of the first theme (as in bars 21–4) played as a simple harmonic sequence with cadences on G$\sharp$ minor, E major, and D major triads, before a sidestep to B major via the fourths figure from bars 69 to 74.

Fifth movement (*Finale*)

Pesante – Presto ($\unicode{x2669}= c.134–146$)

1–49	Exposition	(first-subject group part 1) First horncall and *horă*
50–95		(first-subject group part 2)
96–118		(first-subject group part 3)
119–47		(first-subject group part 4)
148–87		(transition – horncall theme)
188–255		(second-subject group) Second horncall
256–316	Development	(part 1)
317–83		(part 2)
384–417	Recapitulation	(first-subject group part 1)
418–48		(first-subject group part 2)
449–81		(transition)
482–555		(horncall)
556–625		(second group)

Ex. 20   Opening horncall from the finale

1–49 Exposition (first-subject group part 1)

The four-bar horncall theme on F which opens the movement (Ex. 20) can be compared to the naturally tempered melodies of the Transylvanian shepherds, played by the women and young girls on Alpine horns called *bucium*, which Bartók collected in December 1910 in the Turda-Aries region of Romania.[13] The tonality immediately shifts away from F, to an implied D, with an extended *perpetuum mobile* section which appears to be built on A as a dominant. Unusually, this section contains an almost literal transcription of a Rumanian dance called a *horă nemtsească*,[14] which was not collected by Bartók, but was taken from a disk of popular Romanian music given to him by Constantin Brăiloiu. As was stated in the second chapter, it was not Bartók's practice to make use of actual folk material in his major works, preferring to create synthetic folk-inspired melodies. Bartók's orchestra attempts to imitate the sounds and instruments of a Romanian gypsy band (*taraf*), whose members are solo fiddle (*primas*),[15] a kind of two-string guitar (*zongora* or *cobza*) and a plucked bass. The melodic contour of the violin parts circles the pitches of the germinal motif, the sixth note of which has been raised by a semitone to A4, producing a six-note octatonic segment (Ex. 21). During the gradual crescendo from *pp* to *ff*, each subsequent violin part enters in parallel motion (bars 12, 16 and 21), eventually forming what is effectively a decorated dominant minor-ninth chord of D.[16]

From bar 17, the lower group of divisi second violins moves mainly in contrary motion to the upper voices. Against the regularity of the violins, the basses and timpani play a constantly changing régime of metric organization using only E and A, the root and fifth of $A^{\flat 9}$. At the expected resolution of

Example 21. *Horă* theme (bars 8-11 second violins)

the dominant preparation at bar 44, the climax of the section presents a parallel series of chords shifting from G♯ minor, through F♯ major, on to E♭⁷, against a rising whole-tone figure, and an end to the continual semiquaver motion.

50–95 (first-subject group part 2)

A reiterated second-inversion chord of C major, underpinned by a series of rising scales, acts as a new dominant preparation. Most of these scales are derived from an acoustic scale on C, as is their sequence of starting pitches (C, D, E, F♯, G, B♭, C, D and F♯). This time, however, the expected cadence does appear, with a tonic F in bar 59, the *horǎ* melody being adapted to an acoustic scale on F, and rhythmic vitality being supplied by the shifting patterns of the horns. The section reaches its high-point at bar 74, with similar material to that used at bar 44. Here it is considerably extended into a melody influenced by another Romanian dance (the *Mǎrunțel*),[17] which comes into full flower from bars 418 to 429 of the recapitulation. The dance is characterized by the use of a rhythmic figure involving a pair of semiquavers and a quaver, and has a close family likeness to peasant dances from many other regions. It appears to have been a personal favourite of Bartók's, and examples of its idiosyncratic rhythm are found throughout his music. A major hiatus appears between bars 86 and 87 with a low loud B, followed by eight bars which attempt to reinstate the *horǎ* rhythm, punctuated by shrieks from the upper woodwinds. Bars 88–9 can be seen as a model with three types of event: a staccato C♯ minor chord preceded by grace notes in the woodwinds; a descending four-note pattern in the bass instruments; and a rising-scale figure in the strings which articulates the first five notes of the germinal motif. This model is then repeated (the violins' scale passage now outlining the first seven notes of an octatonic scale on D), and extended in a second repetition.

96–118 (first-subject group part 3)

In a more subdued passage, woodwinds pass around a new diatonic variant of the first subject, which, from bars 99 to 108, is harmonized cyclically in two sequences (G⁷–C–F⁷–B♭–E♭, and C–F⁷–B♭–E♭⁷), before the arrival on a G pedal at bar 108. This suddenly and unexpectedly shifts to a B♭⁷ chord (112), which appears to be reinterpreted as a German sixth in D (B♭–D–F–G♯) as it progresses to a chord of A major in the last bar of the section.

119–47 (first-subject group part 4)

The *horă* melody, in its acoustic-scale guise, is passed to and fro from woodwinds to strings. Throughout, the string version stays fixated on F, whilst the winds attempt to reorientate it, first to A, then to D. There is another sudden shift, however, and from bar 137 a chord whose pitches are A, D and G is reiterated by the brass against a chromatic segment (E–F–G♭–G) in the strings and upper woodwinds.

148–87 (transition – horncall theme)

The key of A♭ is initially asserted by the subject of a five-voice fugato based on the opening horncall, employing entries which undermine A♭ by successively appearing a perfect fifth higher (a little like the opening movement of Music for Strings, Percussion and Celeste), before dissolving on to a tranquil melody, which is a varied inversion of the figure in G♭ (not the expected G). The first bassoon transforms its inversion (bars 171–5) into an almost completely pentatonic reinterpretation of the horncall, leading to a further side-stepped cadence in E rather than A♭. A tremolando succession of chords in the strings contains only vestigial traces of the horncall – another example of Bartók's use of the technique of thematic liquidation – and the section ends on a pentatonic chord of A–D–G–C–E.

188–255 (second-subject group)

The enormously extended first-subject group is complemented by a compact second subject, whose tonality is unambiguously D♭ major (which in Lendvai's system is a subdominant key), with a brief excursion on to the flat mediant (F♭ enharmonically notated as E major) between bars 221 and 230. It is propelled by a bagpipe-like melody with a narrow ambitus orbiting F_5, which is first played by the woodwinds, before being passed to the strings at bar 196 to form a further *perpetuum mobile*. There are five basic strands in the texture: brilliant semiquaver patterns in the upper strings; reiterated D♭ and A♭ crotchets in the upper woodwinds; a sustained drone of D♭ and A♭ in the bassoons; a symmetrical repeated ♩♪♩♪♩ ostinato in the cellos and basses; and superimposed on these a new pentatonic horncall figure in the trumpets,[18] which has been likened to the horncalls of the Slovakian swineherds and cowherds of Hont, which Bartók collected in 1910 (Ex. 22). The metrical

Ex. 22   The second horncall figure

organization of this passage places a second-level upbeat on the first bar of the horncall (halfway through the ostinato figure), creating an odd dislocation between 'theme' and 'accompaniment'. At bar 211 the new horncall is inverted by the first trumpet, as if in response to its first presentation. From bars 231 to 243 the D♭ triad has a flattened seventh superimposed, suggesting a dominant function, yet when the chord does 'resolve', it is not on to the prepared G♭, but on to an ambiguous chord which coalesces C major and E♭ major, over a pedal G in the timpani.

256–316 Development (part 1)

The tempo reduces to *Un poco meno mosso*, and the tonality moves to B major, for a regular four-voice tonal fugal exposition on the horncall (Ex. 22) which is preceded by an extraordinary and delicate texture redolent of Balinese and Javanese *gamelan* music. Bartók was familiar with the work of the ethnomusicologist Colin McPhee, a specialist in Indonesian music, and included in his piano-duet repertoire an arrangement of his *Balinese Ceremonial Music*.[19] According to Lenoir these ten introductory bars involve a similar acoustic organization to that of the *gamelan* orchestra; the melody being played by the first harp, the *Pokok* (fundamental notes) by the second harp, and the gongs being imitated by the divided first violins.[20] The fugato which follows is equally bizarre, for Bartók combines high-art contrapuntal techniques with the slightly tipsy performance style of a village band.

317–83 Development (part 2)

The regularity of the first half of the development breaks down in this section, which superimposes multiple rhythmic diminutions of the second horncall melody (starting in minims, then crotchets, then quavers and finally semiquavers), each successive entry being one semitone higher (bars 317–24), a strategy repeated in inversion from bars 325 to 332. A transitional passage from bars 333 to 343 decorates a pair of falling fourths (C_6–G_5–D_5), before descending to E for the next contrapuntal subsection in which two sets of imitative entries (woodwinds and harps) overlap every bar, also repeated in inversion (but without the harp entries). The strings finally settle on a grinding chord containing the pitches D, B, F, G♯ and C♯, the final inversion of a dominant minor ninth in F♯ (C♯–E♯–G♯–B–D).

384–417 Recapitulation (first-subject group part 1)

One's normal expectation for a symphonic recapitulation would be for a restatement of the first subject in the home key, but this is not immediately forthcoming. Instead the lower strings recapitulate the opening of the *horă* melody *pianissimo* in F♯, against which the timpani accents the opening three notes of the second horncall in augmentation (each note is now extended to six crotchet beats). Without any further dominant preparation, the music shifts to the tonic F at bar 394, the regularity of the *forte* semiquavers in the upper strings being counterpointed with irregular quaver groupings in the horns and lower strings. As unexpectedly as the previous change of tonality, the music briefly settles on a *fortissimo* F♯ minor triad in bar 408, before setting off again, and running up through an octatonic scale to a C♯ major triad at bar 412, and hence to a series of repetitions of the notes B♭, C, D and E, a whole-tone segment which acts as a kind of dominant preparation for the climax at the beginning of the next section.

418–48 (first-subject group part 2)

The material of this section is akin to the Romanian *Mărunţel* whose intimations were first heard at bar 44.[21] At the end of bar 429, a four-bar phrase implying A♭^{7} appears, with reiterated dyads in the woodwind, and scurrying semiquavers in the strings (rather like the passage from bars 52 to 58 in the exposition), which briefly resolves on to D♭ (bar 436), before being repeated in harmonic sequence (E♭^{7} to A♭). A second sequential repetition, beginning with an implied B♭^{7}, and forming part of a general decline after the climax, fails to resolve on to the expected E♭, and the section ends on a suspended first-inversion chord of B♭^{7} over which the horns intone a falling octave.

449–81 (transition)

This curious transition, which starts very quietly, has relatively little material in common with that of the exposition, for now only the first notes of each successive phrase in the first violins (D, C, A, G and E) hint at the first horncall's melody. Apart from the D in bar 449, and the A which starts the next phrase at the end of bar 453, the melodic notes are all harmonized with major triads, linking the passage back aurally to the one which terminated the second subject in the first movement. The second half of the transition (bars 469–75) presents an oddly cinematic 'dissolve', in which open-position augmented triads played by the woodwinds move towards each other in contrary motion and combine on an augmented triad (last triplet crotchet of bar 471), the process being partially repeated from bar 472 with minor sixths rather than triads in the rising sequence. Slow-moving pedal notes which have been supporting the texture, moving through the pitches D, A, G, F♯ and G, finally settle on A at bar 480, with E♭, G and B in the upper voices.

482–555 (horncall)

The tonality moves to A♭ (supported by yet another pedal), and the tempo to *Più presto*, for a superimposition of the first horncall played by the bassoons and bass clarinet in long notes as a kind of cantus firmus, against rapidly moving figures (initially using the acoustic scale) in triplet quavers in the strings. At bar 498 the horncall disappears, and the strings take up the 1:3 model scale which was such a feature of the slow movement, against a pedal F♯. The two-bar pattern set up at bar 498 is repeated once, before being altered in conformation at bar 503, allowing it to be subjected to a series of sequential repetitions, against which fragmentary variants of the first horncall are played. By bar 515 the bass has moved up to C and the trumpets and trombone reveal a new horncall (C, G and B♭), played against swirling string lines. At bar 533, the scales transmute again, now to whole-tone formations, providing a moment of harmonic stasis against which the trumpets, then trombones intone the descending opening of the second horncall. As Bartók draws the music inexorably to its climax, the scales remain fundamentally whole tone, the texture being studded with fragmentary references to the horncall. The section ends dissonantly on a *forte* chord bounded by a tritone E♭ and A and a moment of silence.

556–625 (second group)

The second horncall is now recapitulated climactically *fortissimo* in augmentation in F by the brass, surrounded by waves of brilliant scale figures (a mixture of 1:3 model, diatonic and synthetic scale forms), and a descending bass line. At bar 573 a new theme appears in three-bar units (characteristic of some new-style Hungarian, and a number of Serbo-Croatian folk songs), with a falling chain of alternate major thirds and minor seconds (1:4 model) underpinned by a rising Dorian scale on F,[22] a derivative of the first horncall. Its six bars are sequentially repeated a fifth higher at bar 579, and a third sequence a further fifth higher is begun at bar 587, but is disrupted by the addition of a bar to the first phrase (588). A new rising sequence is split between strings and woodwinds reaching E♭ in bar 594, and hence via F♯ and D to a long held G. At this point the original version of the score rapidly finishes through a short descending sequence over a rising scale segment B♭–C–D–E♭–F. On Koussevitzky's suggestion Bartók prepared an alternative ending which extends the closing sequence by eleven bars through variation and repetition, landing on a cymbal crash and trilled C in the strings at bar 615. At this point he takes the opportunity of a final reference to the second horncall, now reduced to C–F–F–A♭–F, in the brass, and an ascending shape $(F_2-C_3-F_3)$ in the timpani. Rapid rising Lydian F scales bring the movement to its brilliant close.

6

Musical analysis

Strategies of integration

Much energy has been expended by Bartók scholars in the attempt to explain the apparent coherence of a music whose sources and techniques are extremely heterogeneous. Most stress the unity of his mature compositions, observing a higher-level synthesis of the various elements which contribute to its surface, especially those features which originate in folk musics. Such a synthesis, it has often been argued, is 'organic', implying a harmony of form and content, in which foreground events are the 'natural consequence' of deeper structural features.

It should be clear from the synopsis that the most immediate and striking features of the Concerto which seem to promote unity are the germinal motif whose contour is found in almost all of the important themes, in one form or other, and the perfect fourths shape first articulated at the start of the *Introduzione*. The evolution of the germinal motif in the introduction to the first movement is carefully controlled, from its first suggestion in the entirely chromatic figure encompassing a perfect fourth between C_5 and F_5 played by the first flute in bar 11. Its function here is twofold: to act as the completion of the first violins' ascent (which only reaches E_5 before falling back to C_5), and thus shadow the opening fourths in the lower strings; and to move the register a fourth higher for the second statement at bar 12. Underneath the flute figure, the cellos and basses play a long held pedal C#, the first of a series underpinning bars 6–54 which forms the sequence C#–F#–D#–E–G, a transposed reordering of the first five pitches of the germinal motif (C#–D#–E–F#–G). The flute meanwhile continues its ascent through fourths from C_5 (bar 10), through F_5, to $B\flat_5$ at bar 21, presenting a hugely augmented rendering of the opening three pitches of the cello and bass lines. The continuation of the figure to an expected A♭ does not appear, though given that it is in the appropriate register, it is possible to imagine the E♭ in bar 58 as the next stage in a cycle of perfect fourths (Ex. 23).

From bar 51 the violin lines playing the *verbunkos* theme (Ex. 10) become

Ex. 23 Overlay of basic pitches of the flute line and pedal notes from bars 1 to 58. This is not in any sense intended to be a 'Schenkerian' graph, though the bracketed notehead is felt to be less structurally significant than the other notes

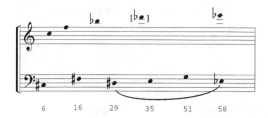

increasingly studded with fragments from the germinal motif, and at bar 56 an unambiguous E–F♯–G–A–B♭ appears, followed by an ascent from A to E♭ to a climax (bar 58) and the start of the last phase of the introduction. The final eighteen bars are completely dominated by the figure E♭–F–G–A♭–A, the 'major' version of the germinal motif, which appears at the recapitulation of the first subject (bar 488).

The arrival of the first theme of the Allegro vivace has been carefully prepared during the introduction, and the foreground features are to some extent mirrored by deeper-level structures. Indeed the opening three bars of this theme itself (see Example 11) can effectively be seen as a summary of the motif developments of the introduction, conflating the pitches of the germinal motif, and those of the interlocking-fourths idea, in a figure which spans three rising perfect fourths (F–B♭–E♭–A♭).

This discussion illustrates an analytic method which seeks coherence through the working out of abstract processes, rather than by reference to the hierarchical relationships of functional tonality. Elliott Antokoletz proposes just such a theory of Bartók's music in which 'diatonic as well as octatonic collections, whether employed as the basis of traditional folk-like themes or as abstract scale patterns, primarily function as pitch sets . . . independent of traditional major–minor harmonic roles'.[1] These sets are 'unordered', containing the pitches of, say, a C major scale, but without the organizing concept of a tonic or 'goal'. Thus, for Antokoletz, the individual themes of the Concerto are manifestations of underlying abstract (or perhaps even ideal) forms – the individual sets – and the unfolding of the work is about their interaction and interpenetration. He regards the first three bars of the Allegro vivace theme as having two constituents, one which is octatonic (F–G–A♭–B♭–B), and one which is diatonic (C–F–E♭–A♭),[2] and suggests that the processes of the first movement involve their extension, and assimilation into

67

each other. For example, from bar 248 of the development, the diatonic fragment is extended to A–C–D–E♭–F–A♭, part of an octatonic collection.[3]

An explanation of the coherence of Bartók's music so entirely divorced from the conventions of tonal function may seem perplexing to some readers. As was noted in Chapter 2, Bartók makes it clear that he conceives his music as essentially tonal, both on a local and a global scale,[4] although its surface is often densely chromatic, because of the superimposition of different modes sharing the same tonic (so-called polymodal chromaticism). Paul Wilson's analytic approach makes use of some of the features in the music which appear to be analogous to those of functional tonality, especially events which are initiatory or imply closure. Graphs of the musical 'middleground' – roughly comparable in appearance to those of Schenker, though also using pitch-class set notation – intended to show the skeletal framework that the foreground (the music we 'hear') elaborates, are 'plotted' from the extracted features in order to demonstrate the movement's integrity. It has already been shown that the pedal notes of the introduction use the same basic set of pitches as did the first bar of the Allegro vivace theme: it would therefore be intellectually, if not musically, satisfying to discover that the whole first movement was also an articulation of the set. Wilson's graph of large-scale structures does not, however, reveal this:[5]

On this scale the important connections are primarily in the bass. The upper voice displays many local structures of interest, but does not show any systematically inclusive design drawn from one of the usual categories. Nor does the bass itself present a single clear-cut design. Instead, each of the three large sections of the sonata form, along with the introduction, provides a single structure of its own.[6]

What Wilson's graph does seem to suggest, is that the first movement is primarily concerned with a relationship based on the interval of the augmented fourth (between F and B), rather than the perfect fifth more normally found in such graphs of tonal music; this perhaps strengthens the claim of B to be seen as a substitute for the dominant.

This clearly conflicts with Lendvai's axis theory, which distributes three basic tonal functions (tonic, subdominant and dominant) to the twelve pitches of the chromatic scale, so that, in the tonality of F, the tonic axis contains F–A♭–B–D, the subdominant axis contains B♭–D♭–E–G and the dominant axis contains C–E♭–F♯–A. Table 1 indicates some of the main tonalities of the work, and isolates their functions according to this theory. This Table suggests that if the functions ascribed by the axis system are equivalent to their normal tonal function then the work has a number of peculiarities: all the movements,

Table 1 Some of the main features of the Concerto tabulated according to the tonal functions ascribed by Lendvai's axis system.

Movement	Section	Tonality	Function
1	Introduction (58–75)	E♭	Dominant
1	Exposition – First subject	F	Tonic
1	Exposition – Second subject	B	Tonic
1	Climax of the development	A♭	Tonic
1	Recapitulation – Second subject (1)	A	Dominant
1	Recapitulation – Second subject (2)	G	Subdominant
1	Recapitulation – First subject	F	Tonic
2	Main tonality of movement	D	Tonic
3	Main tonality of movement	C♯	Subdominant
4	Main tonality of movement	B	Tonic
5	First subject 5–43	A	Dominant
5	First subject 50–8	C	Dominant
5	First subject 59–73	F	Tonic
5	Second subject	D♭/E	Subdominant
5	Development (opening)	B	Tonic
5	Recapitulation (opening)	F♯	Dominant
5	Recapitulation (394–425)	F	Tonic

except the third (which is tonally ambiguous anyway), are in the tonic; the second subject is exposed in the tonic and recapitulates in the dominant and subdominant successively; the second subject of the finale is in the subdominant; and the development section of the finale is for much of the time in the tonic. None of this necessarily invalidates the axis system,[7] but it does suggest that, if it is applicable to Bartók's music at all, his conception of form must differ in a number of ways from common practice.

In actual fact, however, Bartók may have consciously regarded the note lying an augmented fourth above the tonic as a replacement for the dominant in some of his music. The evidence for this statement comes from his own analysis of the first movement of the Fifth String Quartet, in which he remarks:

The first theme has two principal degrees: *B flat* (tonic) and *E* (dominant-like); the beginning, middle part, and end of the movement produce the following tonalities: *B flat*, *E*, and *B flat*.[8]

If B has a dominant function rather than a tonic one in the Concerto, then the second-subject group in the exposition of the first movement and the development of the finale both become located in the dominant area, according with more normal expectations of sonata form. The dominant tonality of the fourth movement resulting from this reading would also make sense, the whole movement forming a kind of dominant upbeat to the finale – a suggestion supported by the bracketing together of the last two movements in the original concert programme. There may be more reason to accept Lendvai's other substitutes, which lie a minor third either side of the conventional tonic, dominant or subdominant. Whatever the case, the whole-tone progression formed by the tonalities of the second subject and the recapitulation of the first subject of the first movement (B–A–G–F) is almost certainly a conscious feature of the work's design, rather than a fortuitous event, for Bartók seems to have been enthusiastic about the use of such 'hidden' deep-level structural features – in the first movement of the Fifth String Quartet, for instance, the tonalities of the individual sections form a complete whole-tone scale (B♭–C–D–E–F♯–G♯–B♭).

The golden section principle and temporal integration

Lendvai's other major contribution to Bartók scholarship, the golden section principle, seems as unhelpful to an understanding of the form of the Concerto for Orchestra, and its individual sections, as is the axis theory. He suggests that the proportional (spatial) concept of the golden mean is applicable in the temporal frame of music, and that major points of change or transformation are to be found at golden sections.

Golden section is subject to three conditions:

   (a) It fulfils its task only if it can be perceived.

   (b) It appears as an organic element of musical *dramaturgy*.

   (c) It represents an *idea* (being the symbol of organic existence).[9]

In the course of the Concerto, few such points seem to lie at significant junctures: in the first movement they lie around bar 95 (after the bar's rest in the first subject),[10] and at bar 248 (beginning of the 'octatonic' stretto); and in the second movement, the major section lies at the restatement of the A section (bar 164).[11]

For Lendvai, 'an analysis is justified only if it leads us closer to the authentic interpretation of music'.[12] This rather disturbing statement further emphasizes the underlying idealism of his position, for if, as may be the case, some of Bartók's forms do conform to golden section principles, what are we to do with this information? Are we to assume that this manifestation of a ratio which is sometimes found in the natural world is an indication of some aesthetic quality? Is an 'authentic interpretation' (the term interpretation being as appropriate to the listener as the performer) one in which we are consciously aware of the proportions of the music? If this is the case, it suggests a mode of listening dependent upon an awareness of the passage of chronological time, rather than the fluctuating, personal 'psychological time' which usually holds sway in the apprehension of music.

Strategies of harmonic integration

When viewed from the more local and less abstract level, Bartók's harmony retains some reliance on tonal methods, albeit in an attenuated form, despite its chromaticism. Example 24, taken from bars 45 to 52 of the third movement, illustrates some of his harmonic practices. This passage, which appears to have a transitional function, involves a two-bar figure repeated sequentially a perfect fourth higher, and a second varied sequence eventually leading to a cadence on a B major triad. Each of the first four bars (45–8) implies a specific triad (F, A♭ minor, E♭, D♭ minor) which is decorated with ambiguous non-harmony notes, in a progression which retains residual traces of cyclical harmony in the motion from A♭ (a substitute for F) to E♭ and thence, via B♭ at the beginning of the fourth bar, to its harmonic substitute, D♭.[13] From the fourth quaver of bar 49, the lower voices outline a descending parallel series of second inversion-triads (D♯ minor, C♯ minor, B major, A major–minor, A♭ minor, G♭ major and F major). Similar passages of parallel motion, which may betray vestigial traces of the influence of Debussy, are found throughout the Concerto, forming points of correspondence.[14] The final quaver of the sixth bar presents pitches which, apparently as the result of contrapuntal motion, together form an augmented sixth chord in B♭ (G♭–B♭–D♭–E). This formation resolves on to the dominant chord of F (with a suspension on B♭),

Ex. 24   Third movement, bars 45 to 52

but instead of then progressing to the expected B♭ triad, it lands a semitone away, on B. Both this final cadential figure, and the overall progression, thus move from F to B (tritone partners), suggesting a kind of dominant to tonic motion.

There is relatively little fully-fledged cyclic[15] harmony in the work, the most outstanding example being the harmonization of the 'Vincze' theme in the fourth movement, where its function is both to characterize the popular style of the melody, and to act as a foil to the near-stationary harmony of the first idea.[16] For the most part, Bartók alludes to tonal practice without fully conforming to its norms, in such a way that he is able to generate in the listener certain expectations of conventional resolution which, however, he often frustrates. A simple example of this is found in the extended passage from bars 5 to 43 of the finale, in which what appears to be a dominant-type chord is prepared, but fails to resolve on to the expected D at bar 44, passing (via G♯ minor and F♯) to an E♭[7] chord instead. This interruption is followed by a second, shorter dominant preparation on C[7], which does fulfil expectations by resolving on to F at bar 59.[17]

The integration of scale forms

Bartók makes use of an astonishing range of different scale forms in the course of the Concerto, most of which are identified in Table 2. Each of these scales has its own specific characteristic features which the thematic material

Table 2 Scale types used in the Concerto for Orchestra
with example locations.

Scale type	Number of notes	Example	Location
1:5 model	4	B E F A♯	(III, bar 106)
Pentatonic	5	F♯ A B C♯ E	(I, bars 1–11)
Synthetic	5	B C♯ E F♯ A♯	(IV, bars 1–20)
Whole tone	6	C D E F♯ A♭ B♭	(II, bars 87–90)
1:3 model	6	C E♭ E G A♭ B	(III, bar 10)
Diatonic (modal)[18]	7	B C♯ D E F♯ G♯ A	(I, bars 501–2)
'Acoustic' (folk)	7	A♭ B♭ C D E♭ F G♭	(V, bars 482–3)
Octatonic (1:2)[19]	8	G A B♭ C D♭ E♭ E G♭	(I, bars 258–60)

generated from them will tend to express. In many cases they share common properties, and attention has already been drawn to the way that the two elements of the first subject of the first movement are transformed by each other's generating scale. It might be expected, however, that such a plethora of scales and modes would be a source of fragmentation and disunity rather than coherence. Of course, Bartók's technique of polymodal chromaticism means that often several different diatonic modes will be superimposed seamlessly, but the particular characteristics of the 'model' scales, and the whole-tone scale in particular, make their integration difficult to achieve. In a sense the entire recapitulation of the finale is concerned with the attempt to fuse many of these scale forms, so that their features are elided.

This process is illustrated in Example 25, a four-bar section of the first-violin line from bars 489 to 492 of the finale. It is accompanied by the second violins, violas and cellos playing parallel transposed versions starting on $A\flat_3$, $G\flat_3$ and C_3 respectively, forming four-note whole-tone segments on every triplet quaver. In the pages which follow this passage, 1:3 model scales are succeeded by whole-tone, diatonic and octatonic formations, which start to coalesce from bar 549 as the movement moves to its final peroration. Over the last five bars (in the final version), the strings and woodwinds play an ascending Lydian (white-note) scale of F, which rounds the work in an assertive gesture that retains the distinctive feature of most of the main themes of the Concerto: a prominent tritone.

Ex. 25   Overlapping scale segments from Movement V, bars 489–92

Strategies of disruption

Whilst it is clear from the anecdotal evidence of listeners' value judgements of the Concerto that it is coherent, in that it seems to produce a satisfying and rounded experience, it is also clear that many listeners, including Hermann Hesse (see above, p. 1), hear within it the imprint of chaos. Such a view cannot simply be dismissed as the naïve interpretation of the musically illiterate, for many sophisticated listeners seem to share the same response.[20] At the very heart of the work lies an interruption, in the often misunderstood fourth movement. For one early critic, Cyrus Durgin of the *Boston Globe*, this movement seemed entirely superfluous:

> The Concerto aspect is served by the treatment of the instruments, while the surviving sense of symphonic structure is established by the first, second, third and fifth movements. That intermezzo is a sort of dalliance . . . along the way.[21]

The interruption is disturbing for a number of musical reasons, but it is perhaps the extra-musical implications which are so significant. Many critics regard Bartók's music as autonomous, untainted by external factors, a view typified by Otto Gombosi:

> To an almost Mozartean degree, his art was detached from his outer life. Autobiographical facets will hardly tempt the future student of his musical output.[22]

The fourth movement clearly has a political and moral function, its impurity fracturing the autonomy of the work, forcing one to reconsider the implications of the entire Concerto. It is certainly not a movement which is concerned with synthesis or reconciliation, despite certain motivic similarities between its constituent materials (the 'Vincze' and 'Shostakovich' themes being related by inversion), and the conversion of the *Leningrad* Symphony theme into a folk-song form.[23] Ironically, the climax of the interruption (bars 103–4) involves the kind of cadential progression described in the previous section as being a particular fingerprint of the work, that of the sharp subdominant (or flat dominant) to tonic: in the passage leading up to this cadence, the prevailing tonality is E♭, but the dominant chord at the end of bar 103 resolves to E major. Thus, one of the apparently integrative features of Bartók's harmonic language, the B♭–E tritone, becomes the crux of the interruption. Although the underlying tonalities of the movement – B, G and E♭ – are related by their membership of an augmented triad, which could possibly be seen as a further unifying element, the three themes of the movement remain melodically, harmonically, rhythmically and texturally distinct, and no attempt is made to reconcile their differences in any kind of false synthesis.

Strategies of formal disruption

Of the other four movements, it is probably in the first that the fracture is felt most strongly, despite all the unifying thematic and tonal features. This comes about partly because of Bartók's superimposition of two formal types, sonata and ritornello rondo, the former being dualistic, and the latter monistic in nature. Throughout the synopsis it was assumed, following the composer's own explanation, that the first movement was in a straightforward sonata form. It is possible, however, to regard the presentations of the Allegro vivace theme which begin at bars 76, 231, 313, 386 and 488 as structural pillars in a ritornello form of the type one might expect in a concerto grosso, and the symmetrical organization of the movement which places the recapitulation of the first subject at the end of the movement reinforces this reading.

Bartók's attitude to musical form was briefly mentioned in Chapter 3, where his tendency to note the durations of each of the individual sections of each movement was observed. He did not do this with the intention of highlighting proportional relationships, however: generally the durations were taken from timings of actual performances,[24] perhaps indicating the pedantic side of his nature as performing and broadcasting artist. What is important, however, is the fact that he was aware of the compartmentalized nature of his works, in which sections tend to be detached from their neighbours, in terms of tempo, texture and orchestration, notwithstanding overlapping elements which help to give the impression of continuity. At times he almost seems to be working with what later came to be called *blocs sonores*, particularly in the third movement, where static 'night music' is juxtaposed with equally immobile pseudo folk song. His own description of the second movement as a 'chain of independent short sections', and the third movement also being chain-like, seems to confirm such a view, which appears to be antipathetic to an 'organic' notion of form, perhaps giving the impression that he was more concerned with a kind of mechanical mould-filling, than the creation of the illusion of 'natural growth'.

It is not entirely clear, however, what is meant by 'natural growth' in music. Growth in living organisms is something we are rarely able to observe; in fact the most we can generally hope to do is sample discrete stages in a process and extrapolate the missing links. Biological processes rarely conform to the highly idealized notions applied by the music analyst, however, or obey simple mathematical formulas such as the Fibonacci series or the golden section; 'natural' growth and development are contingent upon many environmental factors, and may be subject to periods of stasis followed by periods of intense activity, rather than gradual and steady transformation. 'Nested'[25] or recursive structures of a type which may interest 'organic' analysts are, however, to be found in fractal objects, which are as common in the inorganic world (for example, smoke plumes, coastlines and clouds) as the organic (for example, ferns and cauliflowers). In such objects surface features are reflected in a statistically similar way, layer upon layer, in the deeper structure, 'always the same, but not in the same way'.[26] It could be argued that it is the surface disruption of Bartók's music, rather than its deeper-level integration, which gives it a living, vital quality, for biotic processes themselves are often equally discontinuous, fragmentary, and at times apparently chaotic.

Strategies of rhythmic disruption

Bartók's use of folk-song models as replacements for more conventional types of phrase structure has already been noted, and some writers, especially Lendvai, have stressed the extent to which this alien material is seamlessly absorbed into his musical language, in a higher-level synthesis.[27] There may, however, be an irreconcilable strain between the two types of music, the rounded nature of the folk song acting as a brake on the work's forward momentum. In the introduction, the presence of the continuous quaver motion in the lower strings from bar 35 counteracts the potential inertia of the two folk-like melodies, although the distinct changes of texture and orchestration between the three sections accentuate their demarcation. Often, however, Bartók deliberately disrupts the regularity of folk-derivative material by rhythmic changes whose effects are similar to that of extrasystoles ('missing' heart beats) – temporary and short-lived disturbances which can have profoundly disquieting effects. The first subject of the exposition presents an interesting example of this: the first two bars are ambiguous, for there appear to be two possible simultaneous metrical interpretations, 3/8 and

Ex. 26   The opening of the Allegro vivace theme rebarred in 4/4

3/4, the second of these being implied by the syncopation on the second quaver of the second bar (which is lengthened by a dot). When the third (2/4) bar appears, the situation is made even more confusing, for we now seem to have a latent 4/4 bar split into a 3+3+2 Bulgarian *aksak* rhythm (Ex. 26).

By the end of the consequent (bars 79–81), we have become accustomed to the metric irregularity, and if this was one of the *Dances in Bulgarian Rhythm* from *Mikrokosmos*,[28] our expectation of a consistent 3+3+2 rhythm would be fulfilled. However, from bar 82 Bartók changes the metre to a regular 3/8, and reduces the material of bars 79–81 to a skeletal seven-quaver transposition of the consequent (F_5–$D\flat_5$–$B\flat_4$–G_4–C_5–A_4), a quaver shorter than expected. The orchestral interjections help little in isolating the metre in this passage, if anything the hemiolas between bars 84 and 89 confuse the situation even more by suggesting 3/4. Only in bars 90 and 91 do the quasi-perfect cadence and the repetitions of the four semiquavers–quaver figure in the woodwinds finally clarify it as 3/8, yet even this regularity is shortlived, for it is immediately disturbed by an empty 2/8 bar (94).

From bar 95 a new melody with an entirely regular and unambiguous 3/8 metre appears, but this presents a second and more important type of disruption, involving the grouping of bars (the hypermetre). The first phrase seems to be divided into two parts, the first of which is four bars in length,[29] the second (beginning with the characteristic Hungarian quaver–crotchet figure) which is three bars long. The opening section of the next phrase (bar 102) is, however, extended by one bar (105) to make a 5+3-bar arrangement. The following two phrases are in six-bar units, and are based on a three-bar figure which is a rhythmic reduction of the previous phrases (see Ex. 27). When the woodwinds overlay this triple hypermetre with a two-bar figure derived from the main Allegro vivace theme (from bar 123), a curious kind of higher-level polyrhythm is created. Effectively the whole first-subject group is thus destabilized by this dual process of the establishment of a regular rhythmic model and the subsequent disruption of it.

An analogous disruptive process appears at the beginning of the finale, where the strings initiate the ostinato-like Romanian *horă*, against which timpani and

Ex. 27   First movement, bars 110–12

double basses reiterate an E_3 in the rhythm illustrated in Figure 2 (the Figure should be read from left to right and line by line). The rhythmic model (top line) is played, then repeated with one additional crotchet in the third bar. The expectation of a third, perhaps varied, repeat is aroused, but what actually appears is a series of truncated versions of the model which conserve some features while discarding others.

In much of the exposition of the first movement, a norm is established of three-bar phrasing, which is often obscured by the addition or subtraction of individual beats or bars. Whilst three-bar grouping is by no means an unknown practice in earlier art music, it is generally somewhat unusual.[30] An interesting example can be found in the Menuetto of Mozart's G Minor Symphony, K550, where the opening of the first section is articulated as two three-bar phrases,[31] and its completion as two four-bar phrases. Folk songs which proceed in three-bar sections are found widely in both the Hungarian and Serbo-Croatian repertoires, and it is possible that melodies from the latter group, which Bartók had recently been transcribing, could have influenced his writing in the Concerto. Some of these songs exhibit the same combination of three-bar grouping with metrical irregularity which is such a feature of the themes of the first movement (Ex. 28).

Once a three-bar process is established Bartók is at liberty to disrupt it by the occasional addition or removal of bars, or by the temporary change of the higher-level metre. The interplay between different higher-level interpretations becomes particularly prominent in the third section of the development

Fig. 2   Timpani and bass rhythm from bars 8 to 20 of the finale

Ex. 28 Serbo-Croatian song no. 10a
Uranijo bego Omerbego in Bartók's simplification[32]

of the first movement (bars 313–96), where triple (317–34), duple (342–7) and quintuple (349–64) hypermetres succeed each other, before plunging into virtual chaos at the section's climax. The ensuing recapitulation both elucidates the situation (the first reprise of the second subject is in regular three-bar phrases in 3/8 throughout), and confuses it (in its second reprise it is in four-bar phrases). It is symptomatic of the metrical ambivalence and ambiguity of the movement that the last eight bars leave the situation unresolved; the tutti quavers at the beginning of bars 514 and 516 seeming to suggest a two-bar interpretation, which is then disrupted by a cadence figure across the last two bars retrospectively implying a three-bar grouping.

The second movement is characterized by an interplay between duple (or quadruple)[33] and triple[34] hypermetres, but its surface is much less fragmented by the process than was the first movement. The subsequent three movements tend towards the normalization of even grouping of bars, suggesting an overall process in the Concerto which moves from the domination of triple hypermetres in the first part of the work to that of duple ones in the second half.[35]

The Concerto and compromise

There is a certain misunderstanding inherent in this strange situation of a musician who dies in poverty and destitution and is then posthumously promoted to the front rank of 'comprehensible' composers. For, after all, Bartók only found such a receptive audience some years after his death, and one might add that the most admired works are often the least good, the ones which come closest to the dubious-taste, Liszt–gypsy tradition; and his better works are liked for their weaker traits – one thinks of the strolling fiddler and neo-classical aspects. So his work at present conquers by its ambivalence: an ambivalence which is sure to cost him rebuffs in the future when his audience is able to profit from a greater distance of time. . . . His language lacks that internal coherence which might offset an imagination so fertile in short-term invention.

As for the use of folksong in such a directly assimilated and even most nobly authentic form, this is no more than a residue of the upsurge of nationalism in the nineteenth century.... Whether in that brutal violence which animates a 'molten sound material', or in that general calm suffused in a shimmering, rustling halo, Bartók is incomparable at those moments where his poetic genius grants him a truly effective realization.[36]

Pierre Boulez's estimate reflects the modernist community's opinion of Bartók as a potentially radical figure who capitulated to convention, and accepted the route of compromise rather than pursuing the implications of such works as the Violin Sonatas and the middle pair of String Quartets to their logical conclusions. He was, according to Boulez, the 'last representative in the spontaneity of his talent' of the 'old musical world whose contradictions he could never quite overcome',[37] by implication, unable fully to assume the mantle of a 'modern' composer, and unwilling to abandon the bourgeois audience totally, if necessary, in defence of his music's autonomy.

Bartók differed from his major contemporaries, Schoenberg, Stravinsky, Webern and Berg, in one fundamental respect: for much of his life he earned his livelihood as a professional performer, and his relationship with concert audiences was therefore of a different and more direct kind than theirs. It is probably fair to suggest that the simplification of his style in the Concerto was the culmination of a process which began around 1930 with the *Cantata profana*, and continued through the major works of the thirties – from the Second Piano Concerto to the Violin Concerto and the *Divertimento* – and involved, among other things, a reassessment and reintegration of some of the features of the petty-aristocratic *verbunkos* tradition. His sensitivity to the difficulties that audiences had with some of his music is illustrated by a comment in a letter written to Ernő Südy, in January 1934, about a programme to be given in Békéscaba for the Aurora Circle's Bartók Festival:

the piano sonata would give the audience a fright, so there would be no sense in putting it in the programme. But to you (and anyone else who might be interested) I would gladly play it in private (before or after the concert).[38]

It could be argued that, given his parlous financial position, he needed to write a successful composition which would generate sufficient revenue to provide some kind of support for his wife and family after his death. To be successful with the American public, the piece would need to compete with such works as the symphonies of Koussevitzky's hero Shostakovich, and in particular the Fifth and Seventh Symphonies, which were widely performed at the time. However, the circumstances of the composition of the Concerto suggest that

Bartók viewed it more as a personal, visionary statement than a pot-boiler, though he was clearly delighted with its (relative) popular success.

Although there was a four-year hiatus between the Concerto and his previous composition, the Sixth String Quartet – the last work he completed in Hungary – his musical language was little changed. A continued resurgence of latent functional harmony is found throughout the Quartet, including: implied cyclic progressions (I 93–8 C–F–B♭–E♭–G♯–C♯); sequential progressions (I 126–31); parallel progressions (I 222–5 C♯^{7}–D^7–D♯^{7}–E^7); and pseudo-cadential figures (I 312–20 C♯^{7}–F♯). Many of Bartók's other personal fingerprints can be seen in this quartet, such as: harmonically static, but rhythmically mobile ostinato passages (I 180–93); parallel voicings (I 302–10, II 36–42, 115–20, 122–30, IV 55–8); synthetic old-style peasant music (the *horă lunga* which forms the 'trio' of the March);[39] and the emulation of popular performance styles in the March and Burletta movements. There is, perhaps, a greater textural continuity in the Quartet than the Concerto, which is probably a result of the more restricted range of colouristic possibilities.

In the light of this discussion, the specific features of the Concerto which are, for René Leibowitz, particularly characteristic of the slide into compromise, will now be considered more fully.

When Leibowitz objects to 'the continual symmetry of phrases and periods' he probably means their regularity and balance as much as their literal symmetry,[40] but it is certainly true that near-symmetry does play an important role in the melodic shaping of the Concerto, particularly in the first movement, where most of the thematic ideas consist of wave-like gestures which balance rising and falling elements. Indeed, the first musical utterance of the *Introduzione*, the pentatonic figure in the cellos and basses, involves just such a symmetrical gesture; but, as is generally the case in the Concerto, it is a symmetry in which the two halves balance but are not the same. One could equally consider the ostinato figure set up at bar 35, the opening and continuation of the first subject (bars 76–81), the interlocking-fourths idea in the trombone (bars 134–41), the beginning of the development (bars 231–42) and the development of the second subject (bars 272–6) among many other examples of this phenomenon in the first movement. Bilateral symmetry is, however, a fundamental feature of Bartók's musical imagination, and its influence is found at every level, from the large-scale structure of works through to the melodic and rhythmic configuration of themes, even, at times, their orchestration – for example the 'wedge-like' shape of the upper string parts in bars 6-10 of the *Introduzione*. To this extent his music could be said to have fractal-like construction. His most novel aural invention, the 'night music' movement, is saturated with scale forms that are selected because of their symmetrical possibilities. Yet, strangely, what attracted him in folk music was absence of formal symmetry: he generally rejected the new-style 'architectural' songs in favour of older, more irregular, asymmetrical models.

In referring to 'the stereotyped use of the superimposition by contrary motion of the same motif from a tonal centre (first movement)', Leibowitz appears to be considering the passage at the beginning of the *Introduzione*: the string lines move apart in contrary motion forming a kind of turn, which he sees as an example of the mechanical application of a formula which is decorative rather than functional.[41] However, the figure can clearly be seen to have several important musical functions: to assert a secondary tonal centre (C); to outline the whole-tone scale; and to present explicitly the symmetrical motion which lies at the heart of the movement.

Leibowitz's next objection is to 'the parallel motion of a similar melody for two instruments always following a single vertical interval without the change of interval affecting the rest of the harmony (second movement)'. Instances of such writing have already been mentioned with reference to the Sixth String Quartet. Although the same interval is maintained throughout each section (for example, a sixth) its modality is subject to change between major and minor versions. The effect of the doubling in this movement is more timbral than harmonic, however, and it is probable that Leibowitz sees this as an example of the 'impoverishment' of the music which came about through Bartók's abandonment of the kind of 'oblique' polyphony used in the Third and Fourth Quartets, for fundamentally traditional triadic harmony. In any case, thus to criticize a movement called *Giuoco delle coppie* is excessively solemn!

For Leibowitz, the fourth movement exemplifies 'the "decorative use" of a popular melody without functional relationship to the rest of the thematic material'. It was suggested above that the interruption actually does have a thematic and tonal relationship with the rest of the material, but its function is intended to be disruptive and discomforting. For a moment Bartók raises the mask of musical autonomy, and communicates in a way he normally spurns, by means of exogenous signification. The Shostakovich/Lehár melody with its spinning, fairground atmosphere is certainly an alien element, but most definitely not a decorative one.

Leibowitz's final assertion is of 'a general loss of real harmonic control, or rather, a chaotic harmonic structure which ignores for most of the time the recent developments in this domain'. His allegiances were sworn towards

Schoenberg and his school, and he held Stravinsky and the neoclassicists in particular disdain. The recent developments he alludes to were those associated with Schoenberg's 'emancipation of the dissonance' and his subsequent development of the twelve-tone method. For Leibowitz, these testify to Schoenberg's freedom, for he had the choice, when standing at the border of atonality, of standing back and reverting to traditional forms of musical expression. When Bartók stood at the same portal, he chose retreat rather than progress, compromise rather than integrity.

It is particularly ironic that Leibowitz should characterize the harmony of the Concerto as a manifestation of the loss of harmonic control, for this same argument was equally advanced against many of the atonal and serial works to which he gave his support. His objection is particularly to Bartók's retention of the principles of supposedly moribund functional tonality, even if in a restricted form, which inextricably ties the work to a debased aesthetic. This objection can possibly be countered by invoking Lévi-Strauss's concept of a 'first level of articulation, which is as indispensable in musical language as in any other, and which consists precisely of general structures whose universality allows the encoding and decoding of individual messages'.[42] The hierarchically organized scale, which is an invention of culture and not a natural phenomenon, provides just such a general structure, upon which second-level articulations ('expressive' pieces of music) can be founded. Lévi-Strauss argues that the serial method eliminates this first level, compelling the system of signs to be constructed on a single level, which causes the music to become 'unhinged' and fragmented, often perceived for its timbre alone – 'a natural stimulant of sensual feeling'.

It could be suggested that Bartók, faced with the prospect of 'freedom', looked across the boundary into Schoenberg's promised land and imagined he saw in it, not a country flowing with milk and honey, but a desolate landscape planted only with the bitter seeds of inarticulate anarchy. He certainly believed that 'real' atonality did not exist at all because of

that unchangeable physical law concerning the interrelation of harmonics and, in turn, the relation of the harmonics to their fundamental tone. When we hear a single tone, we will interpret it subconsciously as a fundamental tone. When we hear a following, different tone, we will – again subconsciously – project it against the first tone, which has been felt as the fundamental, and interpret it according to its relation to the latter.[43]

If he had been given the opportunity to counter Leibowitz's accusations,[44] he might have argued that his real point of compromise was in those pieces which the modernists held up as his masterworks, the Violin Sonatas and the Fourth

Quartet, where he approached the abandonment of tonality, and that the Concerto for Orchestra was in fact the more logical and consistent consequence of his musical developments.

Bartók and chaos

Interestingly, both Hesse and Leibowitz used the term 'chaos' in conjunction with the Concerto: the first in a positive sense, the second critically. The commonplace view of chaos as disorder has more recently been displaced by a scientific theory which sees within very complex 'random' behaviour, structures of order. As a theory it provides

a new way to think about order, conceptualizing it not as a totalized condition but as the replication of symmetries that also allows for asymmetries and unpredictabilities. In this it is akin to poststructuralism, where the structuralist penchant for replicating symmetries is modified by the postmodern turn towards fragmentation, rupture, and discontinuity.[45]

Chaos and the associated science of fractals provide us with a potent metaphor for Bartók's art. His is an unstable music with complex and fragmentary boundaries, whose surface features are matched by similar 'deeper' structural properties, in which recursive and reiterative techniques abound, and in which small-scale causes, such as the removal of a bar or a beat, can have much larger-scale effects. Although coherent and unified, the Concerto for Orchestra presents no easy synthesis of the elements of which it is composed; East and West coexist symbiotically, sharing the same musical space, but never fully resolve the tensions which separate them. In his attempt to compose a great, universal concerto-symphony of peasant musics, Bartók has actually written a work in which difference is celebrated as much as consensus, fragmentation as much as unity.

Appendix

(a) Bartók's explanation to Concerto for Orchestra

Published in the Boston Symphony Orchestra programme of 1 December 1944

The title of this symphony-like orchestral work is explained by its tendency to treat the single instruments or instrument groups in a *'concertant'* or soloistic manner. The 'virtuoso' treatment appears, for instance, in the *fugato* sections of the development of the first movement (brass instruments), or in the *'perpetuum mobile'*-like passages of the principal theme in the last movement (strings), and, especially, in the second movement, in which pairs of instruments appear consecutively with brilliant passages.

As for the structure of the work, the first and fifth movements are written in a more or less regular sonata form. The development of the first movement contains *fugato* sections for brass; the exposition in the finale is somewhat extended, and its development consists of a fugue built on the last theme of the exposition.

Less traditional forms are found in the second and third movements. The main part of the second movement consists of a chain of independent short sections, by wind instruments consecutively introduced in five pairs (bassoons, oboes, clarinets, flutes, and muted trumpets). Thematically, the five sections have nothing in common and could be symbolized by the letters *a, b, c, d, e*. A kind of 'trio' – a short chorale for brass instruments and side-drum – follows, after which the five sections are recapitulated in a more elaborate instrumentation.

The structure of the third movement likewise is chain-like; three themes appear successively. These constitute the core of the movement, which is enframed by a misty texture of rudimentary motives. Most of the thematic material of this movement derives from the 'Introduction' to the first movement. The form of the fourth movement – *'Intermezzo interrotto'* – could be rendered by the letter symbols 'A B A–interruption–B A'.

The general mood of the work represents – apart from the jesting second movement – a gradual transition from the sternness of the first movement and the lugubrious death-song of the third, to the life-assertion of the last one.

(b) The Public vs. Bartók: is there really a case?

Newspaper article by Rudolph Elie jr published in the Boston Herald,
3 December 1944

If anyone were to ask the average informed musical person whose music he could get along most successfully without, he would be more than likely to reply "Bartók's" without a moment's hesitation. Even the most advanced musical person to whom Krenek or Schoenberg or Villa-Lobos holds no terrors would – and usually does – hedge on the matter of Béla Bartók after making the customary observation that some things of his are fascinating.

This is not wholly because Bartók is one of the least-performed contemporary composers. A few of his works are done occasionally, at least once anyway. In the past five years in Boston, about four have been performed: six if you include Menuhin's performance of the Rumanian Dances on Wednesday, and the Boston Symphony Orchestra's performance of the Orchestral Concerto on Friday and Saturday. Several of his larger works, of which there aren't too many by the way, have been heard on the radio in recent years, and some have been recorded, notably "Contrasts," two of the String Quartets, the First Rhapsody and various pieces from "Mikrokosmos." So at least there have been opportunities to hear Bartók's music, if not as many as his most ardent admirers would like.

Nor is the lack of enthusiasm for Bartók's music to be explained by its inordinate difficulty, and almost all of it is very difficult. Nor can it be explained by the uncompromising bitterness of the idiom, which is – except in the smaller folk dances and songs – completely dissonant. Dissonance today, certainly, offers no stumbling block to the present generation for the simple reason that it has become consonance to a degree that no one would have believed possible three decades ago.

There are two reasons, it seems to me, for the unpopularity of Béla Bartók's music. The first is because all the larger works convey the impression unmistakably that they are without the milk of human kindness. They are, most people think, arid, formidable, harsh, gloomy, uncompromising, intellectual in the iciest sense, and just plain tedious. There is, everyone will admit, the most vivid rhymical [*sic*] vitality (as witness the extraordinary Dance Suite), but it is plain to be seen that it is not Bartók's primary purpose to entertain, divert, or even move his audiences. He might as well, so far as most of us listeners are concerned, hang a large placard behind the musicians which reads "If You Don't Like This Music You Can Go Home."

The second reason is that it is impossible to accept comfortably the melodic materials of Bartók's music without having known them from childhood. It is easy enough to recognize them, which is to say Bartók's music is abundantly melodic, but it is not so easy with the Italian bel canto heritage which is ours to accept them as "true" melodies. They spring more from the East than the West, and are filled with, as Hugo Leichtentritt has so admirably put it, "fantastic and exuberant turns, strange arabesques, rapid runs, ecstatic trills, dynamic contrasts, sudden changes of time, pathetic accents and emotional outbursts."

Thus the combination of a dissonant idiom, an unfamiliar (if often piquant) melody; a savage, primitive and irregular rhythm, and the composer's own austerity and severity in presenting these materials, results in the almost universal coolness with which Mr Bartók's music is accepted in this country.

Well, now, the question is, has he any future as a composer whose music will appear on distant symphonic programs? His influence, of course, is and will remain great, and his smaller folk dances will indubitably appear on concert programs for years to come, but up until the performance of his Orchestral Concerto, I shouldn't have thought any of his larger works would be revived. But this really marvelous composition has at last brought his previous works into focus so far as the average musical person is concerned by tempering the semi-eastern melodic conception which is his birthright, with the western conception which is our own, and projecting both over an orchestral fabric which is warm and rich and gorgeously detailed. Beginning, now, with the Orchestral Concerto and coming under its spell (as it surely must), the public may well seek Bartók out and find, for the first time, the great musical riches that lie concealed behind the austere facade. They are there.

Notes

1 Introduction

1 Hermann Hesse, *Musik, Betrachtungen, Gedichte, Rezensionen und Briefe*, p. 215. Diary-entry of 15 May 1955, translated by Peter Franklin.

2 'If I were to be asked what role Bartók and Kodály played in the art of our century, I should say: they achieved something that no-one had before their time, the *organic synthesis* of the music of East and West: the 'bridge-building' between Orient and Occident.' Lendvai, *The Workshop of Bartók and Kodály*, p. 9.

3 Péter Bartók, the composer's and his second wife Ditta's son, felt that the works written in America 'indicated a new period in his writing, his crystallized period, as I like to refer to it'. Letter to Agatha Fassett, quoted in Fassett, *The Naked Face of Genius*, p. 357.

4 *BBE* (85), 'Béla Bartók's opinion of the technical, aesthetic and spiritual orientation of contemporary music' (1938), p. 516. In response to the editor of *La revue internationale de musique*'s query as to the general direction of contemporary music.

2 Background

1 *BBL*, p. 82. Letter to Stefi Geyer dated 6 September 1907.

2 In 1916 Bartók became a member of the Unitarian Church in Budapest, in order that his son might avoid compulsory Roman Catholic religious education (a child would have been expected to have been educated in the faith of his father, and Bartók was at that stage nominally a Catholic). He was not, however, a regular church attender. *The Inquirer*, 7001 (30 May 1981). According to Béla jr his father was attracted to Unitarianism because 'he held it to be the freest, the most humanistic faith'. *BR*, p. 31.

3 *BBE* (41), 'The relation of folk song to the development of the art music of our time' (1921), pp. 321–2.

4 *BBE* (13), 'Hungarian peasant music' (1933), p. 81.

5 Leibowitz, 'Béla Bartók', p. 711.

6 *Serbo-Croatian Folk Songs*, p. 20.

7 *BBE* (47), 'Hungarian music' (1944), p. 395.

8 *BBE* (29), 'Gipsy music or Hungarian music?' (1931), p. 206.

9 See Ujfalussy, 'Béla Bartók', p. 43, for a discussion of the 'mass proletarianization of the peasantry' and emigration in late nineteenth-century Hungary.

10 *BBE* (4), 'Folk song research and nationalism' (1937), p. 26.

11 See, for example, Downey, *La musique populaire*, for a survey of the folkloric sources. Gillies suggests that Bartók's musical ideal was 'not so much of internationalism as of integration of foreign ethnic elements within a Hungarian-dominated style' (*BC*, p. 12). Whilst this may be true, the alien elements have a sufficiently destabilizing and decentring effect on the music to render its national affiliations ambiguous at the least.

12 *BR*, p. 150.

13 For example 'Bartók as a comic-opera scientist is not one whit less burlesque than a beplumed and bemedalled General who, in his capacity of Dictator-President, has bestowed all his Orders on himself . . .' *BR*, pp. 151–2.

14 *BBE* (12), 'Why and how do we collect folk music?' (1936), p. 9.
15 Lenoir, *Folklore et transcendance*, p. 211.
16 Both were involved in the discovery of the double helical structure of DNA.
17 See *Serbo-Croatian Folk Songs*, p. 18, for a fuller discussion.
18 *BBE* (41), 'The relation of folk song', p. 328.
19 *BBE* (40), 'The influence of folk music on the art music of today' (1920), p. 318.
20 *BBE* (41), 'The relation of folk song', p. 324.
21 *BC*, p. 26, Béla Bartók jr, 'The private man'.
22 *BBE* (44), 'On the significance of folk music' (1931), p. 347.
23 *BBE* (43), 'The influence of peasant music on modern music' (1931), p. 344.
24 *BR*, p. 219, Zoltán Kodály, 'Bartók the folklorist'.
25 *BBE* (52), 'Autobiography' (1921), p. 409.
26 *BBL*, p. 29, 'For my own part, all my life, in every sphere, always and in every way, I shall have one objective: the good of Hungary and the Hungarian nation.' Letter to his mother dated 8 September 1903.
27 Ujfalussy, 'Béla Bartók', p. 43.
28 See Frigyesi, 'Béla Bartók and the concept of nation and volk in modern Hungary'.
29 *BBL*, p. 29.
30 The Hungarian aristocracy was highly stratified, with a rich upper layer of Magyar nobility and a more impoverished lower layer in the countryside. Kossuth stood for this second group, and promoted 'racial and linguistic Magyarism' rather than claims based on the ownership of land. David Thomson, *Europe Since Napoleon* (Harmondsworth: Penguin, 1966), pp. 217–18. By the end of the century, the aristocracy was divided into the wealthy magnates of the upper aristocracy, a middle layer of landless gentry, many of whom who manned the civil service, and the lower gentry who were often in similar economic circumstances as the peasantry. Frigyesi, 'Béla Bartók and the concept of nation and volk in modern Hungary', pp. 258–9.
31 Gillies, *Bartók in Britain*, p. 4.
32 Szabolcsi, *A Concise History*, p. 56.
33 Elements of the style are occasionally to be found in the works of Haydn, Mozart and Beethoven – for example, in the G minor episode from the finale of the *Eroica* Symphony.
34 *BBE* (52), 'Autobiography', p. 409.
35 Bartók's preferred term means 'aboriginal'; it is interesting to note that he uses biological terminology normally applied to an indigenous animal or plant.
36 Downey, *La musique populaire*, p. 371.
37 Bartók began to view the gypsies as corrupters of peasant music: 'The gypsy . . . plays now for the dances of the peasants, now for the gentlemen; he intrudes his own inconstant temperament everywhere, imports all kinds of foreign music, fuses all these elements, adorning them with flourishes learned from cultivated West European society and plays, finally, dance music in which even the connoisseur of folk music finds it difficult to untangle the strands'. *Rumanian Folk Music*, vol. V, p. 28.
38 Frigyesi, 'Béla Bartók and the concept of nation and volk in modern Hungary', p. 274. As Frigyesi points out, it was the middle and lower gentry who were regarded as the 'folk' not the peasantry (p. 263).
39 Given a four-line melody, structures such as ABCD, ABCC, AABC etc. would be regarded as non-architectural (or non-architectonic), whereas structures such as AABA or ABBA in which the final line was a repetition of the first would be seen as architectural (or architectonic). See Downey, *La musique populaire*, pp. 47 and 64.
40 See *BBE* (46), 'Harvard lectures' (1943), p. 363.
41 Lendvai, *Béla Bartók*, p. 70. Lajos Bárdos, 'Heptatonia secunda – Egy sájastágos hangrendszer Kodály műveiben', *Magyar Zene*, 3–4 (1962–3). Cited in Kárpáti, *Bartók's String Quartets*, p. 127.
42 *BBE* (52), 'Autobiography', p. 410.

43 It was Kodály who suggested that the two works should be heard as a pair.
44 Lambert, *Music Ho*, p. 115.
45 *BBE* (41), 'The relation of folk song', p. 326.
46 *BBE* (71), 'Arnold Schoenberg's music in Hungary' (1920), p. 467.
47 *BBE* (68), 'The problem of the new music' (1920), p. 458.
48 *BBE* (46), 'Harvard lectures' (1943), p. 371.
49 B. Bartók, 'Die Volksmusik der Araber von Biskra und Umgebung', *Zeitschrift für Musikwissenschaft* (Leipzig), 2/9 (June 1920), p. 495.
50 Quoted in Stevens, *The Life and Music of Béla Bartók*, pp. 231–2.
51 *BBE* (57), 'Analysis of the Second Concerto for Piano and Orchestra' (1939), p. 419.
52 *BBE* (85), 'Béla Bartók's opinion on the technical, aesthetic and spiritual orientation of contemporary music' (1938), p. 516.
53 See Lendvai, *The Workshop of Bartók and Kodály*, pp. 15–28.

3 Genesis and reception

1 *BBL*, p. 276. Letter to Dorothy Parrish, 8 February 1939.
2 *BBL*, p. 283. Letter to Dorothy Parrish, 17 May 1940.
3 Otto Gombosi, 'Béla Bartók (1881–1945)', *Musical Quarterly*, 32 (1946), p. 9.
4 Heinsheimer, 'Cortège' from *Fanfare for 2 Pigeons*, p. 109. Hans Heinsheimer was the head of the Opera Department of the Vienna offices of Universal Edition from 1924 to 1938, and an employee of Boosey & Hawkes in New York thereafter. Unfortunately some of his recollections are at odds with other sources, and cannot be regarded as entirely reliable.
5 See Heinsheimer, 'Cortège' from *Fanfare for 2 Pigeons*, p. 113 for a fuller discussion. Bartók initially felt that the recitals were successful – in a letter of 2 April 1941 to Béla jr he states 'Our biggest success so far was in Detroit – the audience seems to have been delighted with the programme'. *BBL*, p. 300.
6 *BBL*, pp. 306–7, to Béla Bartók jr, 20 June 1941.
7 An orchestration of the Sonata of 1937 transcribed in December 1940.
8 In a letter to his son Béla of 2 April 1941, Bartók had suggested that there were 1600 folk epics, whereas in the published collection he states that there are 350 heroic poems, 205 women's songs and 60 miscellaneous songs and pieces.
9 He received further funding for half a year to complete the work thanks to contributions from friends and admirers. A single volume containing seventy-five of these songs was finally published in 1951 by Columbia University Press as *Serbo-Croatian Folk Songs*.
10 Béla Bartók jr, 'Béla Bartók's diseases', *Studia musicologica*, 23 (1981), pp. 427–41.
11 *BBL*, p. 324, to Wilhelmine Creel, 31 December 1942. According to Béla Bartók jr, *ibid.*, his medical attendant Dr Gyula Holló detected symptoms of 'atypical myeloid leukaemia' as early as April 1942 (p. 438).
12 *BBL*, p. 330, to József Szigeti, 30 January 1944.
13 *BBE* (46), 'Harvard lectures', pp. 354–92.
14 Lenoir, *Folklore et transcendance*, p. 112.
15 See Bartók's letter of 28 June 1943 to Wilhelmine Creel quoted in Stevens, *The Life and Music of Béla Bartók*, p. 98.
16 Bartók remarked in a letter of 31 December 1942 to Wilhelmine Creel that 'my career as composer is much as finished: the quasi boycott of my works by the leading orchestras continues' (*BBL*, p. 325). He clearly felt that it was hypocritical and condescending of ASCAP to offer charity when he was ill, given that the musical world it represented had previously ignored his music. ASCAP's impulses were not entirely charitable, however, for it seems that it treated the payments of Bartók's medical and associated expenses as an advance against performing-right payments, which it reclaimed after the composer's death. (Lenoir, *Folklore et transcendance*, pp. 113–14).

17 J. Macleod, *Davidson's Principles and Practice of Medicine,* 13th edn (Edinburgh: Churchill Livingstone, 1981), pp. 575–7.
18 *BBL*, pp. 341–2, to Wilhelmine Creel.
19 Bónis, *Béla Bartók*, p. 232.
20 *BBL*, p. 326, Ditta Bartók to József Szigeti, 23 May 1943.
21 Heinsheimer, 'Cortège' from *Fanfare for 2 Pigeons*, p. 120.
22 *Ibid.*
23 In a letter of 30 January 1944 to Józef Szigeti Bartók writes 'My health suddenly improved at the end of Aug. . . . Perhaps it is due to this improvement (or it may be the other way round) that I have been able to finish the work that Koussevitzky commissioned. The whole of September – pretty well day and night – I worked on it.' *BBL*, p. 330.
24 Quoted in *BC*, Elliott Antokoletz, 'Concerto for Orchestra', p. 527. Kroó (*A Guide to Bartók*, p. 224) quotes from a letter written to Hawkes in August 1943 which indicates that he had started work on just such a piece, but was unable to continue it 'because I had no energy or peace of mind'.
25 Percy M. Young, *Zoltán Kodály: a Hungarian Musician* (London: Percy M. Young, 1964), p. 120.
26 'Concerto for Orchestra', *Boston Symphony Orchestra Concert Program no. 8* (1944/5).
27 Adorno, 'Modern music is growing old', pp. 18–29.
28 Except the concertos.
29 *BBE* (84), 'On music education for the Turkish people' (1937), p. 514.
30 The second movement effectively combines the second, third and fourth movements in a slow–fast–slow ternary structure.
31 *BBL*, pp. 327–8.
32 Quoted by Kroó in *A Guide to Bartók*, pp. 225–6.
33 Side drum, bass drum, tam-tam, cymbals and triangle. The percussion is generally sparingly used.
34 László Somfai, 'The primary sources of Bartók's works', *Studia musicologica*, 23 (1981), pp. 2–66. Bartók's sketches are always associated with specific pieces, according to Somfai.
35 There are three, ten-stave, pocket-sized note-books. The first is published as the *Black Pocket Book*, the second and third are held in the collection of Péter Bartók (*BC*, p. 39).
36 Identical except for the revised ending to the finale.
37 The first edition also gives a tempo marking of Allegretto scherzando instead of Allegro scherzando. According to the preface to the revised edition of the conductor's score, the printed version was originally made from one of the two blueprint copies produced for Bartók (the manuscript having been delivered to the Koussevitzky Foundation). Apparently a small strip had been torn from the top of the relevant page of the blueprint copy used by Boosey & Hawkes, and this obscured the upper part of the metronome mark. The editor misread the number 94 as 74, and adjusted the Allegro scherzando to Allegretto scherzando to compensate.
38 'The title of the second movement is a small problem. On the original manuscript there was no title at the time the blueprint was made; later *Presentando le coppie* was added to the original (not to the engraving copy) and this title is also included in the list of corrections to be made in the engraving. In Bartók's file blueprint, however, we find the title *Giuoco delle coppie* and that title appears in the printed version. This title is believed to be the later thought and is left in the Revised Edition also.' Péter Bartók, Preface to the revised conductor's edition of the score, 1993.
39 'Bartókiana (some recollections)', pp. 8–13.
40 Fassett (*The Naked Face of Genius*, p. 322) incorrectly gives the dates of the first two performances as 8–9 December. In a letter of 30 January 1944 to József Szigeti, Bartók remarks that he believes that the première is due on 17–18 March 1944. It is not known why the performance was put back until December. *BBL*, p. 330.
41 In the programme for the first performance, the fourth and fifth movements of the Concerto are bracketed together. For the second pair of performances, the bracket has been removed.

42 *BBL*, p. 342. Letter to Wilhelmine Creel, 17 December 1944.
43 Fassett, *The Naked Face of Genius*, p. 324.
44 Review by Warren-Storey Smith in the *Boston Post* (2 December 1944).
45 Doráti, 'Bartókiana', p. 11.
46 Péter Bartók's preface to the 1993 revised edition of the conductor's score.
47 Rudolph Elie jr, *Boston Herald* (2 December 1944).
48 Winthrop P. Tryon, *The Monitor* (30 December 1944).
49 Rudolph Elie jr, *The Herald* (30 December 1944).
50 *New York Times* (11 January 1945).
51 According to Gillies, Ralph Hawkes was arranging for the British première to be conducted by Boult. *Bartók in Britain*, p. 150.
52 Ferruccio Bonavia, 'Concerto for Orchestra', *Musical Times*, 86 (November 1945), p. 346.
53 This performance does not, however, appear in the Boosey & Hawkes hire-library list.
54 *Les temps modernes*, 2/25 (1947), pp. 705–34.
55 Leibowitz, 'Béla Bartók', p. 714. My translation throughout.
56 *Ibid.*, p. 731.
57 Adorno, *Philosophy of New Music*, p. 4.
58 Adorno, 'Modern music is growing old', pp. 18–29.
59 Lendvai, *The Workshop of Bartók and Kodály*, p. 9. Mosco Carner presents a similar formulation in his piece about the composer in *The New Oxford History of Music: The Modern Age 1890–1960* (Vol. X): 'he succeeded in an organic fusion of Western art-music with Eastern folk music, bringing all the technical resources of the West to bear upon his native material' (London: Oxford University Press, 1974), pp. 274–99.
60 Elliott Antokoletz, *The Music of Béla Bartók: a Study of Tonality and Progression in Twentieth-Century Music*. Paul Wilson, *The Music of Béla Bartók*.
61 Antokoletz, *The Music of Béla Bartók*, p. 138.
62 Wilson, *The Music of Béla Bartók*, p. 32.
63 This example is based on Downey's *La musique populaire*, Ex. 115, from Four Slovak Popular Songs for mixed chorus (1917).
64 Tibor Tallián, *Béla Bartók: the Man and his Work* (Budapest: Corvina, 1981), p. 228.
65 David Matthews, *Michael Tippett: an Introductory Study* (London: Faber & Faber, 1980) p. 76.
66 Roberto Gerhard, Concerto for Orchestra (score) (London: Oxford University Press, 1965).

4 Synopsis I

1 The dominant axis contains the tonalities G, B♭, C♯ and E, and the tonic axis C, E♭, F♯ and A in the tonality of C. Lendvai, *Béla Bartók: an Analysis of his Music*, notes that the recurrences of the first subject of the first movement form the sequence F (76), D♭ (231), A (313), F (386) and F (488), which in an axis interpretation are tonic, subdominant, dominant, tonic and tonic respectively (p. 103). Whether this functional view of the progression is viable is open to discussion, but the symmetrical aspect of the arrangement is almost certainly a conscious feature of the movement's design.
2 Austin, 'Bartók's Concerto for Orchestra', pp. 21–47.
3 *BBE* (46), 'Havard lectures', p. 367.
4 Durations for Movements I and II correct Bartók's erroneous additions (calculated by adding his section durations as they appear in the manuscript and Boosey & Hawkes' score). His first movement duration is given as 9'48", his second movement as 6'17".
5 Lendvai describes a formation which he believes to be a particular feature of Bartók's music which contains the same pitches as the octatonic scale as an alpha chord. In this case it is seen as the superimposition of two diminished sevenths a major seventh apart (e.g. C♯–E–G–B♭/ C–E–F♯–A).

6 The passacaglia theme from the fourth movement of Brahms's Fourth Symphony also uses this same figure transposed to E (E_5–F♯$_5$–G$_5$–A$_5$–A♯$_5$–B$_5$–B$_4$–E$_5$).

7 Béla Bartók and Albert B. Lord, *Serbo-Croatian Folk Songs*. Interestingly, the Hungarian shepherd's pipe ('long type', five hole) is tuned F–G–A–B♭–B–C, and according to Kodály, the third note is often so tuned flat that it sounds as A♭. (Kodály, *Folk Music of Hungary*, p. 114).

8 *Serbo-Croatian Folk Songs*, p. 61.

9 Lenoir, *Folklore et transcendance*, p. 362.

10 Bartók, *Hungarian Folk Music*, no. 86.

11 Except at the beginning of bar 22, where the basses omit the crotchet C♯ at the beginning of the bar.

12 Its four-part ABAvC structure and its isometry suggest some of the formal characteristics of an old-style song.

13 Throughout the synopsis no distinction will be made in terms of modality, the terms major and minor being inappropriate given Bartók's use of tonality.

14 Bartók identifies two particular styles of performance of peasant music: *parlando rubato* with a freer tempo, and *tempo giusto* in strict time.

15 Compare bars 24–6 and 31–5 of the Quartet theme, with the opening six bars of the Allegro vivace theme.

16 Including the last six pieces of *Mikrokosmos*, and the finale of the Music for Strings, Percussion and Celesta.

17 Schoenberg, *Fundamentals of Musical Composition* (London: Faber & Faber, 1967), p. 58.

18 Lenoir, *Folklore et transcendance*, p. 326.

19 These monodic, profane melodies are distinguished by their narrow range (often just two or three notes), and according to Downey, 'constitute the true foundation of Arab music' (Downey, *La musique populaire*, p. 135).

20 Except for the G at the end of bar 230.

21 By hypermetre is meant the tendency for bars to group themselves in an analogous way to beats within bars.

22 Bartók's marking of bar numbers from 349–64 suggests a five-bar phrasing.

23 Del Mar, *Anatomy of the Orchestra*, remarks that harpists tend to use a pencil for this tremolando, as a metal or wooden beater is often too large and unmanageable to strum rapidly.

24 In fact it is a transposition of the figure of bar 487 up one semitone.

25 No title for the movement was given in the original programme.

26 'Chain' is Bartók's own term for the form of this movement (see the Appendix (a)). Lutosławski more recently used the term to describe 'a structural procedure that aims for unbroken continuity by overlapping strands of material as opposed to the more conventional approach of placing phrases or sections end to end'. Charles Bodmin Rae, *The Music of Lutosławski* (London: Faber & Faber, 1994). The short string interludes between the sections of the second movement of Bartók's Concerto for Orchestra tend to alleviate the musical discontinuity which might result from the juxtaposition of discrete sections.

27 *BC*, p. 530. Antokoletz, *BC*, p. 537 note 1, gives Suchoff as the source of the information about the *kolo* (Benjamin Suchoff, 'Program notes for the *Concerto for Orchestra*', in *Béla Bartók: a Celebration* (New York, 1981), pp. 6ff). For similar passages of parallel sixths see the Sixth String Quartet III/78–9, IV/55–8.

28 *Serbo-Croatian Folk Songs*, p. 63.

29 Compare especially the figure in bars 77–9.

30 Except for a small number of chromatic neighbour-notes, the harmony of the subsection from bars 52–5 is derived from a whole-tone formation founded on C (C–D–E–F♯–G♯–B♭).

31 *BBE* (25), 'Some problems of folk music research in Eastern Europe' (1940), pp. 189–90. Also see music example no. 1 from the *Serbo-Croatian Folk Songs* (p. 95).

32 The whole-tone scale is entirely formed from intervals of the major second, and has two forms: C–D–E–F♯–G♯–A♯, and D♭–E♭–F–G–A–B.

33 A rather similar 'chorale-like' passage is found in the fourth movement of the Sixth String Quartet (bars 40–5).

34 Lenoir, *Folklore et transcendance*, p. 358. The English translation of the text reads:

> Come thou of man the Saviour,
> Thou child of a virgin born,
> Mortals over all the world, yea,
> Marvel at Thy holy birth.

35 The correspondences are even closer if the quaver neighbour-notes are ignored.

36 The $E\flat_2$–$A\flat_2$–A_2–D_3 figure initiated by the cello is called the Z cell by Antokoletz, *The Music of Béla Bartók*, pp. 71–2 (in this case Z–3/9) – the term originally deriving from Leo Treitler.

37 Downey, *La musique populaire*, pp. 146–7. The passage also recalls the music associated with the 'Lake of Tears' (the sixth door) from *Duke Bluebeard's Castle*.

38 These arpeggios articulate chords which are called hypermajor or hyperminor respectively by Lendvai, *The Workshop of Bartók and Kodály*, pp. 409–14.

39 The timpani parts are unusual in that the timpanist is instructed to simultaneously play rolls on two timpani rather than a roll between them.

40 Aeolian E, Lydian F, acoustic G, Phrygian G♯, acoustic G, Locrian B, Ionian C, Mixolydian D, and Aeolian E.

41 Del Mar, *Anatomy of the Orchestra*, notes the ambiguity of Bartók's notation – the slurred pairs of semiquavers are normally played as a glissando from the first to the second, but this is not clear from the score.

42 Lenoir, *Folklore et transcendance*, p. 336. My translation. See, for instance, Bartók's *Rumanian Folk Music*, vol. V (Maramureş County), 20a, p. 54, whose text is:

> From the road that you have taken
> There is no hope of returning.
> Where they are about to put you,
> There's no plowing and no carting,
> Neither blows the summer wind;
> There's no tilling with the plow,
> Nor will wind upon you blow. (p. 211)

43 This chord contains the notes G♯–C♯–B–F♯–B♭–E♭.

5 Synopsis II

1 Doráti, 'Bartókiana', p. 12.

2 The German Stiefelträger could equally mean 'tankard carrier'. Stiefel means both boot and boot-shaped tankard.

3 Presumably the trombone glissandi bars 90–1.

4 F. Fricsay, *Über Mozart und Bartók*, Edition Wilhelm Hanson (Copenhagen and Frankfurt am Main, 1962), pp. 59–61. My translation assisted by Peter Franklin.

5 Lenoir, *Folklore et transcendance*, p. 348. My translation.

6 Downey, *La musique populaire*, p. 404.

7 These five notes can also be seen as being extracted from an acoustic scale on E or from B major.

8 Lenoir, *Folklore et transcendance*, p. 432.

9 Bartók uses pedal timpani to provide the bass line in this section, requiring considerable skill from the performer, for as Del Mar, *Anatomy of the Orchestra*, suggests, he seems to have taken little care sorting out the logistics of the pedalling.

10 Lendvai, *The Workshop of Bartók and Kodály*, p. 656.

11 First performed in the United States on 19 July 1942 by the NBC Symphony and Toscanini.
12 It may be, as Bónis suggests in his article 'Quotations in Bartók's music', pp. 355–82, that Shostakovich was himself parodying the Lehár melody. Given Koussevitzky's admiration for Shostakovich, it seems particularly odd that Bartók should choose to lampoon the Seventh Symphony.
13 For this and many of the other folk-references in this chapter see Lenoir, *Folklore et transcendance*, pp. 371–421. According to Bartók (*Rumanian Folk Music*, vol. V, p. 23) this instrument is called the *tulnic* in this region.
14 Lenoir, *Folklore et transcendance*, p. 395. It is also similar to the *Jocul fecioresc* (161c) from *Rumanian Folk Music*, vol. V, p. 147.
15 Bartók even adopts the instrumental technique of repeating notes on the open strings whilst playing a melodic line (see second violin lines, bars 36–43).
16 The initial set of pitches can also be seen as an acoustic scale on A (A–[B]–C♯–D♯–E–F♯–G).
17 A dance of the Romanians of southern Bihor which literally translates as 'mincing'. Bartók's description of the dance appears in *Rumanian Folk Music*: 'The boy and the girl stand opposite each other, the boy dancing as if performing a solo dance. . . . The girl, however, performs neither steps nor motions; she does not even look at her beau and seems rather annoyed by all this "showing off". One wonders whether this peculiar behaviour of girls may not be the remains of a very ancient village etiquette, according to which the girl has to show a neutral or concerned – if not an averse or contemptuous – air in the face of any attempted courting by the boy', pp. 40–1. Fassett describes Bartók's attempt to teach her the dance.
18 Except for one note, the B♭ in the penultimate bar.
19 Balinese music also influenced piece number 109, from vol. IV of *Mikrokosmos From the Island of Bali*. See *BBL*, p. 319, for a concert programme including the McPhee transcription.
20 Lenoir, *Folklore et transcendance*, p. 393.
21 This melody can also fruitfully be compared to the *Jocul nepoatelor* or 'granddaughters' dance' of Maramureş county. See, for example, *Rumanian Folk Music*, vol. V, p. 171.
22 The complete sequence would have been C–A♭–G–E♭–D–B♭–A–F, but Bartók reverses the last two pitches.

6 Musical analysis

1 *BC*, p. 527; Elliott Antokoletz, 'Concerto for Orchestra'.
2 Part of a Phrygian F mode, which emerges forcefully in the continuation of the theme in bars 86–91.
3 The octatonic scale this segment is derived from is A–B–C–D–E♭–F–G♭–A♭.
4 Adorno remarks that during a conversation with him in New York, Bartók told him that 'a composer like himself, rooted in "folk music", would in the end be unable to do without tonality – a surprising statement for a man like Bartók who, in the political sphere, had resisted so successfully any nationalist temptations and had chosen exile and poverty at a time when Europe was plunged into Fascist darkness' (Adorno, 'Modern music is growing old', p. 20).
5 Wilson, *The Music of Béla Bartók*, p. 187.
6 *Ibid.*, p. 186.
7 See *ibid.*, pp. 203–8, for a detailed discussion of the theoretical problems with Lendvai's justification of the axis system.
8 *BBE* (54), 'Analysis of the Fifth String Quartet' (1935), p. 414. In his analysis of the Music for Strings, Percussion and Celesta he describes E♭ as the 'remotest key'. In terms of the cyclic progression of the entries of the subject, it literally is the remotest, for all other 'keys' have been traversed on the way to it. It is not clear that Bartók regards it as being remotest tonally from this statement.
9 Lendvai, 'Remarks on Roy Howat's "Principles of proportional analysis"', p. 257.

10 Using timings rather than the number of bars.

11 By major section is meant the point which lies at 0.618 * total duration, by minor section, the point that lies at 0.382 * total duration.

12 Lendvai, 'Remarks on Roy Howat's "Principles of proportional analysis" ', p. 257.

13 In this case, a movement up through the cycle of fifths. Bars 46 and 48 could be also read as F^{o7} and $B\flat^{o7}$ respectively.

14 I 95–109, 192–223, 456–75; II specifically 105–8, 212–18, but parallel motion is the main generating force throughout the movement; IV 114–18; V 175–87, 370–2, 449–68, 579–87.

15 By cyclic harmony is meant those root-progressions which move through a series of falling or rising fifths – e.g. G–C minor–F–B♭–E♭, or G–D–A minor–E minor.

16 It may also possibly be a tribute to Kodály's Concerto for Orchestra which contains a similar cyclic passage.

17 In traditional harmonic terms, the passage between bars 5 and 59 may be seen as a perversion of the sequence A^7–D–G–C–F in which the second two stages have been replaced by $E\flat^7$.

18 All the modal orderings of the diatonic scale are found in the course of the work.

19 The octatonic scale, when viewed from a western, diatonic point of view, seems to combine two minor tetrachords, whose tonics lie an augmented fourth apart – e.g. F–G–A♭–B♭/B–C♯– D–E.

20 I base this statement on my experience of teaching the work to undergraduate students.

21 *Boston Globe* (25 March 1950).

22 *BR*, p. 209.

23 Whilst the linear shapes are similar, the intervallic content is different in inversion. Lenoir goes as far as analysing it as 7,7,7,7 4) (3) (2 1–9, $Av^4Av^3Av^2A$ – the structure of an old-style folk song!

24 It is not clear from the autograph score when Bartók added the timings.

25 By nested I mean that the same or a similar pattern is repeated on a number of levels of observation.

26 Schenker's motto *semper idem, sed non eodem modo*.

27 Throughout his writings, Lendvai seems to use the term 'synthesis' in its Hegelian sense.

28 The sixth dance involves a 3+3+2 rhythm.

29 It should be noted that Bartók is careful about the placement of bar numbers – invariably they appear at musically important areas such as the beginnings of phrases. In this section they fall at bars 95, 102, 110 and 122.

30 Other examples include the *Ritmo in tre battute* section of the Scherzo of Beethoven's Ninth Symphony, the opening of the Allegro of Mozart's String Quintet in C Minor, K406, and the finale of Brahms's String Quartet in A Minor.

31 The hemiolas in the first two bars of this section produce a wrong footing 2+2+2+3 crotchet pattern over the phrase.

32 *Serbo-Croatian Folk Songs*, p. 114.

33 The important distinction is between odd and even groupings.

34 The B and E sections and the Trio have a very clear triple hypermetre.

35 Though bars 573–87 of the finale have a triple hypermetre.

36 Boulez, 'Entries for a musical encyclopaedia', pp. 241–2.

37 *Ibid.*, p. 242. The sentence is reordered from the original English translation.

38 *BBL*, p. 227, 20 January 1934.

39 Romanian 'long song'.

40 That is, he does not mean that the second half of a phrase or period is the retrograde of the first half.

41 Leibowitz, 'Béla Bartók', p. 727.

42 This and subsequent quotations are taken from Claude Lévi-Strauss, *The Raw and the Cooked* (London: Penguin, 1986), p. 24.

43 *BBE*, p. 365.
44 He had, of course, died the year before.
45 N. Katherine Hayles, 'Complex dynamics in literature and science', in *Chaos and Order: Complex Dynamics in Literature and Science*, ed. N. K. Hayles (Chicago: The University of Chicago Press, 1991), pp. 10–11.

Select bibliography

Adorno, Theodor W. 'Modern music is growing old', trans. Rollo H. Myers, *The Score*, 18 (18 December 1956), pp. 18–29
  Philosophy of New Music (New York: Seabury, 1980)
  Quasi una Fantasia, trans. Rodney Livingstone (London: Verso, 1994)
Antokoletz, Elliott. *The Music of Béla Bartók* (Berkeley: University of California Press, 1984)
  Béla Bartók: Guide to Research (New York: Garland, 1988)
Austin, William. 'Bartók's Concerto for Orchestra', *The Music Review*, 18/1 (February 1957), pp. 21–47
Bartók, Béla. *Béla Bartók Essays* (London: Faber & Faber, 1976)
  Béla Bartók Letters, ed. János Demény (London: Faber & Faber, 1971)
  Hungarian Folk Music (London: Oxford University Press, 1931)
  Rumanian Folk Music, ed. Benjamin Suchoff, 5 vols. (The Hague: Martinus Nijhoff, 1967–75)
  Serbo-Croatian Folk Songs (with Albert B. Lord) (New York: Columbia University Press, 1951)
  'Die Volksmusik der Araber von Biskra und Umgebung', *Zeitschrift für Musikwissenschaft*, 2/9 (June 1920), pp. 488–522
Bónis, Ferenc. *Béla Bartók: his Life in Pictures and Documents*, 2nd edn (Budapest: Corvina, 1981)
  'Quotations in Bartók's music', *Studia musicologica*, 5 (1963), pp. 355–82
Boulez, Pierre. 'Entries for a musical encyclopaedia – Béla Bartók', in *Stocktakings* (Oxford: Clarendon Press, 1991), pp. 237–42
Cooper, David. 'Paul Wilson: The Music of Béla Bartók', review, *Music Analysis*, 13/2–3 (1994), pp. 305–11
Cooper, David, and Henderson-Sellars, B. 'Has classical music a fractal nature? – a reanalysis', *Computers and the Humanities*, 27 (1993), pp. 43–50
Del Mar, Norman. *Anatomy of the Orchestra* (London: Faber, 1981)
Dille, Denijs. *Béla Bartók* (Antwerp: Metropolis, 1974)
Doráti, Antál. 'Bartókiana (some recollections)', *Tempo*, 136 (March 1981), pp. 8–13
Downey, John. *La musique populaire dans l'œuvre de Béla Bartók* (Paris: Centre de Documentation Universitaire, 1966)

Fassett, Agatha. *The Naked Face of Genius: Béla Bartók's American Years* (London: Victor Gollancz, 1958)

French, Gilbert G. 'Continuity and discontinuity in Bartók's Concerto for Orchestra', *The Music Review*, 28/1–2 (1967), pp. 122–34

Frigyesi, Judit. 'Béla Bartók and the concept of nation and volk in modern Hungary', *The Musical Quarterly*, 78/2 (Summer 1994), pp. 255–87

Gillies, Malcolm (ed.). *The Bartók Companion* (London: Faber & Faber, 1993)
Bartók in Britain (Oxford: Clarendon Press, 1989)
Bartók Remembered (London: Faber & Faber, 1990)

Griffiths, Paul. *Bartók* (London: Dent, 1984)

Heinsheimer, Hans. *Fanfare for 2 Pigeons* (New York: Doubleday, 1952)

Helm, Everett. *Bartók* (New York: Cromwell, 1972)

Hesse, Hermann. *Musik, Betrachtungen, Gedichte, Rezensionen und Briefe* (Frankfurt am Main: Suhrkamp, 1985)

Howat, Roy. 'Review article: Bartók, Lendvai and the principles of proportional analysis', *Music Analysis*, 2/1 (1983), pp. 69–95

Juhász, Vilmos (ed.). *Bartók's Years in America* (Washington DC: Occidental, 1981)

Kárpáti, János. *Bartók's String Quartets* (Budapest: Corvina, 1975)

Kodály, Zoltán. *Folk Music of Hungary* (London: Barrie and Rockliff, 1960)

Kroó, György. *A Guide to Bartók* (Budapest: Corvina, 1974)

Lambert, Constant. *Music Ho* (London: Penguin, 1948)

Lampert, Vera, and Somfai, László. 'Béla Bartók', in *The New Grove: Modern Masters* (London: Macmillan, 1984)

Leibowitz, René. 'Béla Bartók ou la possibilité du compromis dans la musique contemporaine', *Les temps modernes*, 2/25 (1947), pp. 705–34

Lendvai, Ernő. *Béla Bartók: an Analysis of his Music* (London: Kahn and Averill, 1971)
The Workshop of Bartók and Kodály (Budapest: Editio Musica, 1983)
'Remarks on Roy Howat's "Principles of Proportional Analysis"', *Music Analysis*, 3/3 (1984), pp. 255–64

Lenoir, Yves. *Folklore et transcendance dans l'œuvre de Béla Bartók* (Louvain-la-Neuve: Institut Supérieur d'Archéologie et d'Histoire de l'Art, Collège Erasme, 1986)

Lesznai, Lajos. *Béla Bartók* (London: Dent, 1973)

McCabe, John. *Bartók Orchestral Music*, BBC Music Guide (London: BBC, 1974)

Milne, Hamish. *Bartók* (London: Omnibus, 1982)

Moreux, Serge. *Béla Bartók* (London: Haverill, 1953)

Somfai, László. 'Manuscript versus Urtext: the primary sources of Bartók's works', *Studia musicologica*, 23 (1981), pp. 2–66

Stevens, Halsey. *The Life and Music of Béla Bartók*, 3rd edn, ed. Malcolm Gillies (Oxford: Clarendon Press, 1993)

Szabolcsi, Bence. *A Concise History of Hungarian Music* (Budapest: Editio Musica, 1974)

Tallián, Tibor. *Béla Bartók: the Man and his Work* (Budapest: Corvina, 1988)

Ujfalussy, József. *Béla Bartók* (Budapest: Corvina, 1971)

Volek, Jaroslav. 'Über einige interessante Beziehungen zwischen thematischer Arbeit und Instrumentation in Bartók's Werk: Concerto für Orchester', *Studia musicologica*, 5/1–4 (1963), pp. 557–86

Weissman, John S. 'Béla Bartók: an estimate', *The Music Review*, 7 (1946), pp. 221–41

Wilson, Paul. *The Music of Béla Bartók* (New Haven and London: Yale University Press, 1992)

Index

Made in the USA
Lexington, KY
21 April 2012